We're back and more hard-boiled than ever.

Call us self-serving, but this time we'd like to thank some of the critics who've supported Old School Books. In case you missed it, here's what a few of them had to say:

Spin: "Walking the mean streets with hearts set on dreams they know damn well they'll never reach, these authors keep it realer than any rapper knows how. . . . They testify to how much was lost when these novelists couldn't get read as seriously as they should have."

The Source: "They take the brutality and ruin of the urban black landscape and transform them into art."

Playboy: "One of the most exciting literary revival series since the rediscovery of Jim Thompson's novels."

Detour: "The Old School will give the modern reader a wake-up slap, alerting them to a subversive canon too long ignored."

Details: "Down-and-dirty tales about real O.G.'s, stories that drop you in the middle of the crumbling inner cities for a street-level view of the black urban experience. . . . If you like the page-turning pulp of Raymond Chandler, James Ellroy, and Jim Thompson, definitely add the Old School to your hard-boiled syllabus."

Time Out: "Unflinching biographies of the streets . . . a blood-soaked landmark of crime fiction."

USA Today: "Harder than a set of brass knuckles and pulpier than home-squeezed orange juice. . . . With any luck the legacy of the Old School Books writers will not be lost again."

New York Newsday: "The editors have unearthed a motherload of revelation; a shadow tradition of hot-wired prose playing its own variations on noir with bebop abandon and rhythm-and-blues momentum."

Kind words, and don't think we aren't grateful.

While we've got your attention, we'd like to make this important announcement. OSB will soon unveil its first hardcover reissue:

Chester Himes's lost classic *Cast the First Stone*. Least that's what the world has called it until now. With a little help from some friends, we've restored one hundred (or so) pages from Himes's original manuscript, "dyed" several of the characters black as they were in Himes's earliest editions, and are publishing it under its original title, *Yesterday Will Make You Cry*. We consider it nothing less than a literary revelation—we hope you will too.

Until then, we hope you enjoy our terrific trio of new titles. And be sure to keep those cards and letters coming.

Man Walking on Eggshells

OLD SCHOOL BOOKS

edited by Marc Gerald and Samuel Blumenfeld

HERBERT SIMMONS

Man Walking on Eggshells

SIMMO

Old School Books

W · W · Norton & Company
New York · London

Copyright © 1997 by Marc Gerald and Samuel Blumenfeld

Introduction to MAN WALKING ON EGGSHELLS copyright © 1997 by Herbert Alfred Simmons. MAN WALKING ON EGGSHELLS copyright © 1962 by Herbert Alfred Simmons. Copyright renewed 1990 by Herbert Alfred Simmons.

The text of this book is composed in Sabon
with the display set in Stacatto 555 and Futura.
Composition by Crane Typesetting Service, Inc.
Manufacturing by Courier Companies, Inc.
Book design by Jack Meserole.

Library of Congress Cataloging-in-Publication Data
Simmons, Herbert.
    Man walking on eggshells / Herbert Simmons.
        p.   cm.—(Old school books)
    ISBN 0-393-31618-1 (pbk.)
    1. Afro-American men—Fiction.   I. Title.   II. Series.
PS3569.I47327M36   1997
813'.54—dc21   97-5673
                                                                         CIP

W. W. Norton & Company, Inc., 500 Fifth Avenue, New York, N.Y. 10110
http://www.wwnorton.com

W. W. Norton & Company Ltd., 10 Coptic Street, London WC1A 1PU

1 2 3 4 5 6 7 8 9 0

To my sister Phyllis Ann because . . .

And to Obie, a true friend, for the
same reason

HERBERT SIMMONS

Johnie H. Scott

With the Old School's publication of Herbert Simmons's *Corner Boy*, a whole new generation has come to appreciate a work *Spin* recently compared to "James M. Cain's lyrical jailhouse existentialism" and *Detour* heralded as "startling in its lyricism and as blunt an indictment of urban American ills as ever reached the American public." We can only assume greater accolades will await the rediscovery of his fol-

low-up, *Man Walking on Eggshells*.

The life and career of Herbert Simmons have enough twists and turns for a Hollywood script writer—all it needs now is the happy ending for which, as you'll see in Simmons's preface, he continues to strive.

Born in St. Louis in 1930, Simmons's mainstream literary career lasted only five years and spawned only these two novels. According to Simmons, "Coltrane and Davis were the most pivotal influences in my writing career. They didn't compromise. That's the reason jazz went the way it went, because these artists found a socially acceptable way of being maladjusted personalities. I did too, but I hit a brick wall while doing it."

The "brick wall" Simmons refers to is the novel you're about to read, which chronicles militant jazz musician (think Miles Davis)

Raymond Douglas's rise from the ashes of East St. Louis. More ambitious and overtly political than *Corner Boy,* as well as more linguistically experimental, its publisher, Houghton-Mifflin, hardly knew what to do with it.

Cut off from the publishing world, Simmons went underground where he became an early member of the Watts Writers Workshop and would fight the power as a member of the Nation of Islam. He subsequently became a professor at California State University at Northridge and a thriving businessman.

By any estimation, Simmons's life can be seen only in terms of resistance, integrity, steely resolve, and ultimately triumph. Still, while Simmons himself would be loath to frame his literary career in this light, one can't help but wonder what might have been had his original publisher seen his writings as they were and not as they wished they'd be.

INTRODUCTION

Still Walking, But Not on Eggshells

ONE HAS TO SEARCH long and hard to find African Americans still alive who had novels published before my first novel, *Corner Boy*, which came out in 1957 when I was twenty-seven years old. I am not at all confident you will find any. During that span, my conviction that an artist must create works reflecting reality has never waned. And so, even now, you'll find me, as they say in the vernacular, "still talking that talk, and walking that walk," but no longer on eggshells.

Check this out.

While in Europe, during the spring of 1996, on a book tour promoted by a Scotland firm (Canongate's Payback Press), I was categorized as a crime writer and I liked that description, because when you think about it, so were William Shakespeare *(Macbeth, Julius Caesar, Othello, Hamlet, Romeo and Juliet)*, Charles Dickens *(Oliver Twist)*, Victor Hugo *(Les Miserables)*, Feodor Dostoevsky *(Crime and Punishment)*, George Orwell *(1984)*, and Richard Wright *(Native Son)*.

Well, my inspiration for writing *Eggshells* was Miles Davis. Back then I was twenty. Miles was three years older and the downest dude I knew in my generation—I had not yet met Malcolm X—but more than that, Miles had made it from the corner, and I surmised, if he could, so could I! Now, you know, I knew I had to get my stuff together, because Miles was master of that blue note and could play it full tone, half tone, quarter tone, you name it—and still capture social nuances of the day. John Coltrane (heavily influenced by Miles, I might add) did the same thing with his formidable "sheets of sound," laying siege to our sensibilities with pulsating dissonance echoing deadly wounds of disparity between our actions and convictions.

So, you see, from the beginning, as a word composer, influenced by Miles, I reflected on reality by using words the way jazz musicians use notes. And so, just as Bird and Diz created bebop in jazz, I was forced (by the nature of what I was doing) to conceptualize and come up with "assimbilationalism." "Assimbilationalism" allows a writer freedom to use whatever literary device, form, style, or movement works, to make a word composition work—whether it's as old as romanticism or classicism, or so young as to be brand new. For instance, I use tense and person the way Miles used time and tone. However, merely improvising is not sufficient. Jazz musicians have to blow soul! And I have to show how people feel and what is really real in my writing. In other words, what I must do is make the prose swing so hard the words sing.

Subsequently, *Eggshells,* though experimental (to Houghton Mifflin's credit, they published it), cuts through the social and publishing taboos of that period while also telling a solid story for the reader.

However, miscalculating the power of the American caste system, the publisher proclaimed, on the inside flap of the back cover of *Eggshells,* that thirty-year-old Raymond Douglas was "an intelligent, gentle boy, walking, as he must always walk, on eggshells." I don't think so! My generation and the generation after me destroyed that caste system, and along the way, refusing to be bogged down in the inertia of bitterness, I pursued the forty-year path that now allows me, as an entrepreneur, to publish my own books and produce my own movies, if I so desire.

And so I stand today, an unshackled being, writing about protagonists who don't believe in integration or segregation, but rather "collective separatism," an oxymoron, coined by myself, meaning "the cohesiveness to come together on matters mutually beneficial to all, but also the freedom that allows us to go our separate ways."

In *Man Walking on Eggshells,* corner boy Raymond Douglas becomes a man when he attacks the American caste system holding him down, rather than directing antisocial behavior against the community within which he resides, in order to style and prosper on a fast lane hillside.

The militant tone of and action in *Eggshells,* though published in 1962, is still too strong for some folks to swallow. However, time moves on, and so must people, willingly or unwillingly. We are living in a new day now, but we are still being challenged by the age-old, universal issue of man's inhumanity to man. And as far as universality is concerned, jazz already wears those credentials. So does "assimbilationalism," especially when related to a thematic structure and plot involved with the inhumane behavior of *homo sapiens. Eggshells* is the first novel of a trilogy that includes *Tough Country,* my latest novel, and *Land of Nod,* a novel-in-progress. This three-volume work, entitled *Destined to Be Free,* chronicles the saga of the Andersons (an African-American family) during their sojourn in slavery and journeys into the space age, which includes a jail break on the moon.

So, as you can see, I am still very much walking, but hardly on eggshells.

H.A.S.
San Fernando Valley,
Northridge, California

Man Walking on Eggshells

. . . he blew like a man walking,
they said. Like a . . .

Part One

Walking

. . . Sunday was for singing gospels and praising God for heaven, but those other six days they shouted the blues . . .

AND THE BLUES DESCENDED like a dull slate sky wrapping around a mountaintop. All over the country the blues descended, all across the nation as the news got around. Florence Mills, symbol for aspirations among ten million people, was dead.

Darkness rolled into St. Louis with the news. Darkness drowned the sun in the sky and washed activity from the streets below. The city stabbed at the darkness with feeble glowing streetlights and rivers of silence flowed from the wound.

"Wake up, Hosea," Mae said, pulling the covers back from around his shoulders.

"Damn, puddin, seems like I just hit the sack."

"You did."

"Huh? Then what the hell you wake me up for then?" Hosea wanted to know.

"I'm scared. It's pitch-black, dark out there."

"Is that all you woke me up for? You been in storms before."

"It's not storm black outside, it's night black," Mae said.

"Aw go on."

"If it's not then I'm not eight months pregnant and you're not the daddy," Mae said.

Hosea got out of bed and came over to the window where she was standing. What he saw out there took his breath away. The glare from the streetlight across the way was shimmering and bobbing through the darkness like a light flashing under water.

"It's twelve o'clock high noon," Mae said. "This sure is the strangest day I ever saw. What do you suppose is wrong?"

"Well, I can tell you one thing," Hosea said. "It ain't just Florence Mills."

They were at the window when bleary water began to bleed from the clouds.

They were at the window when whiplashes of fire silently began to crack the sky open.

They were at the window when the winds came.

And then they knew.

IN THE BEGINNING he was a voice in the wind storming his way into existence.

A half day passed before they dug them out. When they succeeded, even the reporters and cameramen, standing there with their equipment poised, got more than they'd bargained for.

In the beginning he was wind in a storm voicing its way into existence.

After a split second of surprise, cameras snapped, reporters jabbered away, policemen fought back the curiosity seekers pressing to the attack, and a few of the other officers in charge pestered the crowd and victims for the necessary information.

In the beginning he was voice storming wind.

Only after they finished all this vital business did the doctor get the opportunity to go about his affairs.

3

STORK BATTLES TORNADO TO DELIVER BUNDLE OF JOY
TORNADO KID GREETS NATURE'S FURY

"**W**ELL, I'll be damn."

"All right now, mister," the dark, pretty waitress said, giving Wilbur a stern look from behind the counter.

Wilbur looked up with a wrinkle of appeasement on his forehead. "No fooling, look," he said, pointing to the picture in the paper of the baby born in the tornado that had flattened the south side of St. Louis.

"What's biting you?"

"I'm an uncle, yeh, me."

"Well, don't die about it."

He pointed the story out to her, the one about Mr. and Mrs. Hosea Douglas.

"They your kinfolks?"

"I'm trying to tell you?"

"Well, if that don't beat everything. Born in a tornado on the very day that Florence Mills died too."

"Yeh, that's weird, ain't it?"

Marsha nodded. "I hope he don't grow up to be nothing like you," she said smiling at him.

He stood up. "Hey pretty, when you going give me a break?" he said.

"Uh-uh, you don't know how to do right," she said.

"Aw, see there, you talking about me, and I thought you was my friend."

She laughed. "You going to Florence's funeral?"

"Yeh."

"I can't go, I got to work. Why don't you drop by here after it's over and give me the lowdown?"

"I'll do that." He winked at her and went out the door.

She frowned her nose at him.

*A*ND THERE WERE five thousand people inside. And there were one hundred thousand milling around outside Mother Zion Church. And there were one hundred and fifty policemen maintaining law and order. And the crowd flowed like a rhythmic ocean sweeping along everything in its path. And the one hundred and fifty policemen formed a city-dispatched dike to hold them at bay.

Red had a hipflask and he passed it around to Wilbur and Huss. There were other people in that crowd passing gin around too, and some of the old folks gave them disapproving looks and some of the young folks gave them envying looks, but most folks didn't even notice, too intent on trying to get into the church or at least get a glance at what was going on inside. There were some guys out there slashing pants pockets with razorblades too, getting the rent money, and some guys taking advantage of the shoving crowd to get up close to some girl they'd always wanted to.

The police cursed and sweated and thought more about their tired, aching feet than their dignity vanishing as the army of wrinkles invaded their stiffly starched uniforms. Their eyes shifted back and forth uneasily, watching a multitude of dark stirring faces standing out like white petals bordering gigantic charcoal-brown flowers sprinkled with all colors of the spectrum.

SOMETIMES I'M TOSSED . . .

And the crowd splashed around, a dark wave of murky colors dazzling in the sunlight, a reflection of perspiration, and tears held in check by organized confusion. The famous Hall Johnson choir and the congregation communicated.

AND DRIVEN, LORD . . .

They wiped their faces with handkerchiefs, stepped on each other's toes, cursed, and pressed forward against the wall of people hoping to get a glance at Florence before it was too late.

And the policemen looked at their watches. How much longer, goddammit?

Young guys pulled newly found girl friends away from the crowd, or cruised through looking for trouble, snatched hats off dignified old men's heads and beat it down the street, wormed out to the outskirts of the gathering and jumped up and down on car hoods, broke lamppost lights for the hell of it, slashed tires.

SOMETIMES I DON'T KNOW . . .

Then at last the doors opened.

"Here they come!"

"Where?"

"Look, they going to bring her casket out now!"

"Florence." They pointed.

"Florence!"

"Florence!"

"Florence!"

"Florence!"

But of course she was dead and couldn't hear.

"Give us some room, please."

"Watch out there, brother."

They brought her casket out slowly, forcing their way through the dense, shifting mass.

"Please, don't take the flowers off the casket."

"Oh dear, God!"

WHERE TO RO-OOOOOOOOOAM . . .

Eleven cars carrying flowers. Thirty girls from the stage, dressed in gray, a walking escort; the cortège followed.

And there was Bell-Ans for indigestion.

I'VE HEARD OF A . . .

"Florence!"

"Florence!"

"Oh Florence."

The procession forged through, a ship cutting a path through a rough sea, the escort and cortège trailing along in the wake.

On One Hundred and Forty-fifth Street.

Oh God, and now they going out to the graveyard, but she ain't never coming back.

A CITY CALLED HEAVEN . . .

Up in the sky an airplane whined overhead, slowly circling like a giant vulture, waiting.

I'M TRYING TO MAKE HEAVEN . . .

And the airplane circled low, going way down like blues were riding on the wings, releasing a flock of black birds which thundered up and darkened the sky.

5

HEY DIDN'T GIG that night. They ran all over New York having a ball. At one place they hooked up with Tricky Sam's group and Filthy, but they didn't stay long, really not up to it yet, and they went on down and caught Sam Wooding at the Club Alabam and that swinging Chick Webb at the Savoy, aw bro! Talking about blowing, those guys what could you say? That crowd knew it too. They stomped the floor right out from under that place. Some of the older folks were still doing the Charleston, which had been out of style way over a year now. And the flasks floating in that place! Who the hell thought of this prohibition anyway? They ran up against Lippy at the 101 Ranch, but he was just sitting in. He said he had heard so much piano he didn't play anymore. He just sat around and thought piano. And Dickie Wells was swinging like usual, the Lenox Club was doing all right, but in the Yeah Man, you wondered how a place could jump like that and still hold together.

They even got by the Lincoln Theater on 135th and caught the King, Louis Armstrong, but Wilbur didn't try to go up against him. Ethel Waters was there, Snake Hips Tucker, and Butterbeans and Susie. Ole Louis preached a sermon on his horn that touched you to the quick and just about wore your soul-case out. They went around to the little place where Ethel used to gig before she made the bigtime. They had a big, fine-looking gal in there, but she wasn't in Ethel's class. Then they had to go around and hit all the little joints they had missed along the way. By the time they wound up back on Lenox, at 135th, it was three o'clock in the morning and their heads were going around like a spinning top. They leaned against the iron fence with the rest of the guys who had finished their gigs for the night, bunched together like a band of thieves, and talked music, raising hell about who could outblow who and who got cut the last time out.

Wilbur said he had a nephew who had been born in a tornado.

They talked about the fire spitting from the King's horn every time he soloed.

Wilbur said his sister and brother-in-law had made the front page of every daily in the country.

They talked about Joe Smith and that soft felt hat and the things he could do.

Wilbur said his nephew's name was Raymond Douglas.

They talked about Bessie's feud with Ethel.

Wilbur said a tornado had knocked a house down on his sister while her baby was being born and what did they think of that?

They talked about the Duke, they talked about Kansas City and that lady piano player there named Mary Lou who some insisted could cut Lil, and there was a piano man there too called the Count, and a drummer that went by the name of Jo Jones.

Wilbur said to hell with them.

But they didn't go home behind that, hell no. They went on around to Smiley's and sat in and finally got around to what had been eating them all day long. And so they took out their horns and talked about it in the smoky, hush-quiet cellar kept in business by the musician trade who made it by after finishing the gig for the night, and they fingered their instruments, gave voice to their horns and talked about her long after the inky-black diluted to charcoal in the sky, long after the night cold dissolved before the approaching dawn, and long after the early brightness arrived they were still talking about her.

6

Lord, I hate to see that evening sun go down . . .

ST. LOUIS WAS a blitzkrieged city shelled out by nature, and a frosty wind whitewashed battered houses standing against the skyline like broken beer bottles in a pile of trash.

Argustus Anderson angrily kicked the front tire of the pickup truck and to his surprise saw the ancient vehicle sputter, cough, and come to life. Without giving it another thought he vaulted inside, took off across Eads Bridge, and entered St. Louis on the other side of the river where he almost ran into a policeman rerouting the incoming traffic. The cab of the truck was so short he was forced to drive with his legs almost doubled up under his chin although he was only five feet ten inches tall. He arrived over on Biddle Street with the fenders still intact but rattling as though they would fall off at the next bump in the rough street. Argustus bolted to the ground, smoothed down his thick mustache, polished the diamond stickpin on his tie and the watch chain dangling across his vest, adjusted the boxback coat and started for the house. Then he paused, looked down at his shoes, took out his handkerchief and wiped them off until they caught his reflection. Satisfied, he went up on the front porch and knocked on the door.

Banny answered, patting the braid, which formed a circle on top of her gray hair. That was the effect Argustus Anderson had on women. Banny Douglas was sixty-nine years old.

Argustus placed his gray beaver Stetson over his heart and grinned. He still had plenty of black, curly hair although it was starting to gray at the temples.

"Hi, y'all. Well, I'll be durn, Banny, if you ain't getting prettier by the day."

He tried to pick her up and swing her around, but she was too heavy so he settled for shuffling her around in a way that slightly resembled a dance.

"Cut out your durn foolishness now, Argustus, and let me be."

"Where's my best gal, Bertha?"

"Hush your mouth, fool. Fred's goin kill you yet for messing round like that."

Argustus raised an eyebrow. "He ain't at home, is he?"

"Naw, he's at work like all menfolks should be."

Argustus grinned, then Bertha came in the front room with pie dough on her hands.

"Might of known it was you making all that racket down here."

"I was just telling Banny how I'd be pulling those long hours in a packinghouse too if I was married to a woman as pretty as you."

"Argustus Anderson, the good Lord's goin strike you dead one of these days for lying like that."

"Yeh, it looks like he's already done struck him silly, if you ask me."

"Why Banny, honey chile, how you talk."

He put an arm about their broad waists.

"I never could resist pretty girls, and Lord I'll be durn if I can figure out which is the prettiest, mother or daughter."

He puffed on his cigar in the front room, where no smoking was allowed, and dumped ashes in a tray used strictly as an ornament.

"I know somebody who's full of a lot of stuff," Banny said. "As full of it as a Christmas turkey."

"Why Banny, shame on you."

Mae was pouting by the time he got upstairs.

"Thought I'd better come over and have a look at my grandchild," he said.

"Five days after the blessed event, why bother?"

"Now Mae honey, is that the way to talk to your poppa?" He kissed her on the forehead. "Uuu-mmm," he said. "Where's Hosea?"

"In the bathroom."

"Well, let me see that little bugger."

He pulled the cover back and looked at the baby. He had the chocolate complexion of the rest of the Douglas clan, the long bullet head and steel-wool hair of his father.

"Hey, he's got two teeth already."

"His name's Raymond," Mae said. "Raymond Charles Douglas."

"That's a good name," Argustus said.

"We decided we didn't want any juniors, especially any named after you."

Argustus turned to Banny and Bertha. "I thought I taught my kids to have better respect for their elders than that."

Hosea wandered into the bedroom rubbing his eyes. "Hi, Pop."

"Hey, just the man I want to see. I got a pickup truck outside right now to move you in."

"You've got what?" Mae said.

"I got just the place for you too. Everything's been taken care of. This guy I know busted up from his wife and he's got this place over his coalyard—"

"You want us to move into a shack in a coalyard, you must be out of your mind."

"Shut up now Mae, I thought I learnt you to stay out of menfolks' conversations?"

"Well, to tell you the truth, Pop, me and Mae was planning on staying here with my folks until we could get back on our feet."

"That's why I told this guy you'd take this place. See, he just wants somebody to sort of look after it. You won't have to pay no rent and you can get all the coal you can use out there in the yard." Argustus winked. "I got him to throw that in extra."

"They don't have to pay no rent here."

"Yeh, Bertha, but young folks should be off someplace on their own, ain't that right, Banny honey?"

"You doing all the talking."

"See, Banny knows I'm right, now what you all arguing against her for?"

"Who's arguing against Banny for Go—"

"Good, then it's all settled, everybody's got they mind made up."

"Well, chile, I know one thing. You sure got your'n made up," Banny said.

They ended up moving, which didn't take long since most of their furniture had been destroyed by the tornado and all they had to load into the truck bed was clothes and a huge, cabinet-door-styled victrola.

Banny watched through the curtains as Argustus and Hosea got Mae and the baby up front in the cab. Hosea got in the truck bed to watch and see their possessions didn't fall off on the way over to the new home.

"That man, he's a card."

"Chile, you ain't said nothing," Bertha said.

"Stays out all night long fooling around, gambling and smoking and drinking and carrying on something awful with the women-folks."

"Why, Banny, how in the world you know all that? The only place you ever go, when you leave here, is to church."

"It just mortifies my soul the way that man carries on."

"You old hypocrite, you know you like him."

"If'n the devil's that goodlooking, no wonder poor Eve done what she done, poor chile," Banny said.

Bertha just shook her head watching the truck depart, Argustus's cigar disintegrating in a cloud of smoke almost matching the fumes from the truck's exhaust pipe.

The place above the coalyard, on Sixteenth and Morgan, turned out to be pretty nice, with three rooms and a bath, hardwood floors, recently papered walls and the latest modern furniture. All Mae's visions of coaldust on the wood panels vanished. She didn't even put up a fuss when Argustus wanted to take Hosea and go off someplace gallivanting around to celebrate the birth of his grandson.

Hosea was not so indulgent. "What about Mae?" he wanted to know.

"Don't worry, she'll be fine. Women in this family's strong as horses."

"But, she just had a baby."

"Son, let me tell you something. Her maw was up two days after she had Wilbur and one day after Mae was born."

"Yeh, but—"

"Go on and get it over with," Mae said.

"Huh?"

Argustus grinned. "You're the first husband I ever knew'd complain 'cause his old woman let him out the house. I'm going have to have a long talk with you, boy, 'fore you ruin the racket."

Market Street was their first stop. They parked the truck and took to the sidewalks.

All along the blocks people went in and out of the houses. They bought pig's feet, hot tamales and Polish sausage from peddlers shuffling through the streets with pushcarts. They bought barbecue from the tiny smoke-filled plywood concession stands. They bought chewing gum and cigarettes, and dipping snuff, and chawing tobacco, and taffy candy from the corner stores and alcohol and water in Coca-Cola bottles from houses around Market and Johnston Avenue, and they crowded the movie houses smelling of popcorn and hotdogs and unclean toilets.

Argustus and Hosea dropped by the Hollywood Club and sat down at a small table up front where they could look right over the railing at the band. Argustus slipped a half dollar to a fat, jovial waiter for a half pint of whisky, but Hosea wouldn't touch the stuff so Argustus sat there and drank it all by himself.

"I'm beginning to wonder what in hell I got for a son-in-law," Argustus told him.

It wasn't long before Argustus had gotten fed up with the Hollywood Club. According to him the band was terrible. Hosea thought it sounded pretty good, but he figured Argustus knew what he was talking about since he had been a musician himself for over twenty years. Argustus wanted to go over on Compton and Delmar to a place Hosea had never heard of, but first they had to stop off at the coalshed in the alley off Johnston Avenue to get another little drink. Argustus finished the Coca-Cola bottle before they got to Compton and Hosea figured it would be a good idea if he took over at the wheel, but Argustus wouldn't hear of it.

It was just a plain ordinary looking brick house and when they got inside it was so dark you couldn't see a thing for a while. Finally they stumbled down to the end of the hallway and pulled back some curtains. You could hear the piano then and when they got around a little bend there was this huge, dark, baldheaded guy on the piano really balling 'em back. Every now and then he would reach up from the piano with one hand for a glass of alcohol and water and never miss a stroke with the other.

"Hello, Tony."

"How you Mr. Andy?"

They found a place and sat around for a while. "I got him this gig three years ago and he's been holding it down ever since. Nobody else wanted him 'cause he's blind."

"Aw yeh?"

"Yeh, but his fingers see fine if you know what I mean?" Argustus said.

Hosea knew one thing, it was time for him to be getting back home to Mae and the baby.

Argustus wouldn't hear of it. Instead they went over in East St. Louis to meet some of his friends.

East St. Louis smelled like a packinghouse and smoke from the factories filled the air like a fog. Argustus promised to give Hosea all his secrets on how to get along in married life and especially to teach him how to handle Mae. He never did though. He took him to the 201 Club on Missouri Avenue and passed cigars around like Raymond was his son.

Twenty minutes later they were in the back room where Argustus got so wrapped up in a crap game he wouldn't pay attention to anything Hosea had to say.

"Son," he finally said, missing the bar on a point, "I'm real right disappointed in you. You don't smoke, you don't drink. I'm beginning to wonder how in hell you and Mae ever come up with a baby."

After that he wouldn't talk to Hosea at all. Finally Luke came along and Hosea bummed a ride back with him.

"That Argustus, he's a pistol."

"Pistol, hell, you mean a shotgun," Hosea said.

"Yeh," Luke laughed. "With both barrels loaded and firing all the time."

"Yeh."

"He must know everybody in East St. Louis."

"And all the joints."

"Yeh, and I've seen him around a lot in St. Louis too."

"He used to be a musician and got around."

"What he stop for? He ain't but, what—forty-six, forty-seven?"

"Somewhere along in there. I always wondered why he quit playing. I never did get the full story on that."

"Well, he seems to be doing okay."

"He's some kind of agent in the music business. One time he even got some guys a recording contract to put out race records," Hosea said.

"No fooling?"

Luke let him off on Market, around the corner from the coalyard, and they shot the breeze for a few more minutes. "Well, I guess I better dust my broom," Hosea said. "Thanks."

Luke gave him the high sign.

Mae wasn't exactly waiting up for him, but she wasn't asleep either.

"You poppa's a cannonball," Hosea said.

"Shush, you'll wake the baby."

"How's he doing?"

"All he does is eat, sleep and give me a week's washing of dirty diapers a day."

"Poor puddin." He planted a kiss on the high arc of her cheek and started taking off his shoes.

"Your father's really something. I had to bum a ride to get back. If I'd been waiting for him I'd still be in East St. Louis."

"Yes," Mae said. "And if I thought for one split second Raymond was going to turn out to be anything like him I'd go down to the bridge and throw him in the deepest part of the river I could find."

Hosea grinned and started to laugh, until the realization that she meant it stopped him.

THEN CAME THE TIME when snowmen appeared, sporting lump-coal eyes and brooms for hands, and further down, on Market Street, gloveless Santa Clauses crouched beside orange crate fires trying to chisel pennies with metal cups. Brown-faced Santa Clauses, in red flannel uniforms soot-streaked like the coalshed houses, with paper-stuffed cracks, interspersed all over their Market Street.

"Yea coal!" the sound of winter cried in the street, and worshipers beat out "Silent Night" with a tambourine.

All of the Douglases were tall, dark and hefty, except Hosea's mother Bertha and his grandmother Banny, who were just plain fat; but Banny's size didn't keep her from trying to run everything, especially at Thanksgiving and Christmas when the whole family was together.

A pickup truck creaked down the street with men in ragged pullover sweaters sitting on the load of coal in the back. "Yea coal!"

"Chile, you mean to tell me they got fools out there working on Christmas Day?" Banny said.

"Maybe their kids won't have no Christmas if they don't," Hosea said.

Banny put a plump hand on the back of her neck and frowned.

"Humph, chile, that ain't nothing out there but the workings of the devil if'n you ask me."

There wasn't any sense in telling her nobody had asked her either and though she was so religious she went to church every evening, she wasn't above taking a little sip of homemade wine.

Fred had a whole gallon jug of gin which he and his grown sons were drinking. They almost exiled Hosea over with the women because he wouldn't touch the stuff.

Fred slapped him on the back. "Still staying in shape, huh?"

"Yeh, I guess."

"Ain't nothing wrong with that. Lots of times I wish I never got started on the stuff."

"Oh, hell," Joseph said.

"Why you got to keep encouraging him?"

"Well, what's so wrong with that?"

"Ain't nothing going to ever come of it, that's what's wrong with it," Elijah said, "and he's got a wife and baby to support these days, so he ain't hardly got no time for daydreaming."

"Yeh, boy, you been dreaming long enough," Joseph told Hosea. "First you had to go and run off to college. Now what good did that do you?"

"None," Elijah said. "Got him a job in the post office where he's got to slave all night long. Hell, I know a lot of guys clerking in the post office who ain't never even finished high school."

"And now he's running around here with his chest all stuck out talking 'bout he's got to stay in shape 'cause he thinks somebody's going pay they good, hard-earned money to watch him monkey around with a football." Joseph grabbed his brother. "Boy, you been living in a cloud long enough. They got a special place just made for you in this world and it's about time you found out what it is."

"Shut up. Both of you shut your goddamn fool mouth!"

"Fred, what's got in you?" Bertha said.

"Elijah and Joseph, y'all don't hush up that racket I'm gone put y'all out of here."

"Aw Banny!"

* * *

After supper Elijah and Joseph got back on Hosea.

"Well, it ain't exactly no kid game," Hosea told them. "Red Grange made over—"

"Red Grange!"

"Who the hell you think you are, boy?"

"You go on out there and try, boy, you hear me?"

"Yeh, Dad."

"Don't pay no attention to your fool brothers," Fred said.

Mae heard the argument and almost dropped a plate. She didn't want Hosea to play football either, because she was afraid he might get hurt, but when they had finished up out in the kitchen, she went into the living room and put her hand on his shoulder to show him whose side she was on.

"Well, one thing's for sure," Hosea said. "We'll sure have to wait until August to find out."

"I'm just thankful, Lord," Banny said, counting her blessings, "so downright thankful I don't know what to do."

8

ARGUSTUS SHOWED UP New Year's Day so drunk he could hardly stand up, loaded down with presents and apologies for just getting by for Christmas.

He had bought them a radio, and a toy trumpet for the boy.

"He won't have any use for that," Mae said.

"It's only a toy, Mae honey."

"I wouldn't have him seen dead with even a toy one of those things," Mae said.

Argustus chuckled and hugged his daughter until she complained. "How's that one for ya?" he said, winking at Hosea. "A musician's daughter who can't stand the sight of a horn."

Mae made Argustus stay for dinner even though he insisted he had a million and one more important things to do.

Argustus said, "Goddamn that radio."

The radio announcer said the United States had enjoyed the most prosperous year in the history of the country.

And August was a long time coming.

The baby was trying to walk and Hosea couldn't study his scheme, half the time, fooling with him.

That boy was something, a pistol already and not even a year old yet. Hosea liked to throw him up in the air, which scared Mae to death. Not Raymond though; he would keep coming back, grinning and raring for more, until Hosea got tired. Then Hosea would bounce him on his knee and sing songs to him, like—

Fifteen men on a dead man's chest. Yo ho ho and a bottle of rum.

Or

Shave and a haircut, six bits! Who's gonna pay for it? Tom Mix!

But he didn't always want to be bothered with Raymond; like now.

"Hey puddin. You better come and get him. He's done done something."

"Why don't you change him, if that's all it is?"

"That's your department."

"Oh, Hosea, really. Sometimes you make me sick."

She came and got him. "You see how your father treats you? Yeah, he's a fair-weather friend, that's what he is. Yeah, poor baby. Your mean ole father, he don't care if baby poddy's wet."

Hosea took out a handkerchief and wiped the perspiration from his forehead.

"Today's the day, isn't it?"

He nodded.

"Don't worry, honey, you'll make the team."

"Yeh."

But she wasn't any surer of it than he was and he knew it. He didn't eat much breakfast. He sat around and tried to read. Finally he gave that up and went out into the backyard. The alley smelled like rotten eggs and slimy turnip greens, and maggots were growing fat in the garbage cans. Hosea started throwing rocks at the cans, driving the flies off in black, spiraling clouds.

"Hi, Mr. Douglas!"

"Hey, Ricky. You going swimming?"

"Yes sir." The skinny ten-year-old grinned and ran down the alley in a pair of overalls cut off at the knees.

"Boy, you watch where you're going! You don't wanna get glass in your feet!"

Maybe he was a fool wanting to try out for a pro football team? Maybe his brothers were right?

Everybody but Fred thought he had gone off the deep end. He couldn't understand how they could think like that. Hell, this was 1927. Even Mae thought like that. She hadn't fooled him telling him he'd make the team. If you listened to them you'd swear he had no reason in the world to act like that and was wrong as two left shoes.

The flies returned, swarming over a dead rat smashed into a red, tire-rutted pulp by a passing truck. Milk-colored water trickled between the bricks and formed a puddle where the alley dipped. Flies found that too. That was reason enough for him.

"**H**EY, BOY, you looking for something?"

"I'd like to try out for the team."

"You what?"

"This is the tryout camp of the Cougars, ain't it?"

The two fat guys looked at each other.

"Well, boy, now look—" one of them said.

"You're kind of light for a lineman," the other one said.

"I play in the backfield."

"You do what?"

"Give him a suit, Luke."

It was a short, baldheaded guy with a cigar talking.

"Yeh, but—"

"Give him a suit."

The one called Luke shrugged. "Okay," he said. "Come on, you."

After he got his equipment, Luke took him to the locker room. There was a lot of nervous talk going on in there.

"Hey youse," Luke said in his high, nasal twang and the talking stopped. "This boy here's going try out for the team."

Luke grinned and left. All the players began to test their equipment, then one after the other they filed out leaving Hosea in there by himself.

On the way out he bumped into a huge, blond guy.

" 'Scuse me," the guy said.

"That's all right."

His eyes followed Hosea out the door.

"Hey, youse," Luke said when he spotted Hosea coming over to join the group gathered around him, "run back in there and tell that other guy to hurry up and get his fanny out here. I don't want to have to go over all this again."

The blond guy wasn't in any hurry. He took his time dressing. By the time they got outside the gathering had broken up and the backfield was tossing around footballs while the linemen charged each other.

"Where the hell youse guys been?" Luke said. "You goofed round and missed defensive and offensive instructions. That's just too bad for you. I ain't 'bout to repeat them."

The big guy shrugged.

"Hey youse? What's your name?"

"Elmer Jabloski."

"Well youse and your buddy better watch out. Attitude counts on making this team too."

"I play football," Jabloski said.

"What does that mean?"

Jabloski shrugged. "Nothing, 'cept I figure playing football counts more than kissing ass."

Luke turned red. "Youse guys might just as well turn in your suits now." He walked away.

"What you play?" Jabloski asked Hosea.

"Quarterback."

"Come on, let's go over with the backfield. Coach Blakey invited me to the tryouts, not ole lard ass."

Hosea started to say no one had invited him, but he didn't know what would be the point in saying that.

They had trouble breaking into the football-tossing session, at least Hosea did, so Jabloski got a ball and he and Hosea started throwing it at each other. Then the baldheaded guy blew a whistle.

"All you guys who came to try out, come around in front so I can get a look at you," he said.

There were twelve of them.

"I'll consider myself a lucky son-of-a-bitch if I find at least one good player among you," he said, "and I'll be even luckier if the one I find can last over two seasons in this league."

He looked them over.

"In case anybody don't know it, I'm Leon Blakey and I run the show. Now, this here is Mike Cassaers, and this is Craig Luke, my assistants."

The way it wound up, everyone was on a team except some veterans the coach was sure of, and Hosea.

"Jabloski," Cassaers said. "The coach said to put you in as linebacker. Think you can play that?"

"I play football," Jabloski said.

He did too. He could sense what hole the play was being run through and bottle it up before it got started good. He could get double-teamed and knocked flat on his back and he would get up and still make the tackle.

The first time he got his hands on the ball he ripped through the secondary and ran over the safety man without even breaking stride.

"Agh, that ham's just lucky," Luke said.

Blakey smiled and dismissed two tryout hopefuls playing guard. "Hey, kid," he yelled at Hosea. "No sense you hanging round if all you going to do is loaf. Get out there and take Murson's place at safety."

On the first play, after Hosea got out there, Jabloski caught a short, hard one in the flats and headed down the sidelines. He was by the secondary before they even realized what had happened and Hosea had to come all the way over from the far side to get him. He had a good angle on him though and went into him low, driving with his shoulder as hard as he could. Jabloski seemed to take off and fly, but Hosea stopped him two yards out from the goal line. Jabloski's momentum had carried him five yards after his feet were knocked from beneath him.

"Hey, Luke, how 'bout sending us a safety man?"

"Yeh."

"You don't like him?" Blakey said, chewing on his cigar and looking at the linebacker who had started the complaining.

The linebacker looked at the coach.

"You don't like him?"

"Naw, I sure as hell don't."

"Okay," Blakey said, throwing up his hands, "I'll get you somebody else then."

Hosea started off the field.

"Hey, hey kid?"

Hosea looked around.

"You can play right half, can't you?"

"Well, to tell the truth, I really play quarterback."

Blakey tugged at his chin and stuck out his lip. "Okay, Kelly, I don't want to make you look bad so you sit down and let the kid take over for a spell."

St. Louis in August, the hottest month in the year.

The center overshot Hosea and he barely had time to catch up with the ball before the whole defensive line smothered him for a fifteen-yard loss.

"What's the matter, boys?" Blakey said. "You forget how to block?"

He was grinning when he said it, but on the next play the line held. The center overshot Hosea again though, and the ends caught him as soon as he picked up the ball. They slammed him to the ground hard, clean though.

Blakey sent in a new center, and everybody on the sidelines stood by silently watching.

On the next play the left guard crashed, but Hosea was rolling out to pass so it didn't matter. He couldn't find a receiver anywhere on the field though and that really got his goat, but he didn't give up, hell no! He reversed his field and left half of the defensive line strung out behind him. He headed for the sidelines, trying to turn the corner and get through the secondary before the linebackers could come up and stop him. As he took off into high a linebacker managed to get over and block his path. Hosea broke stride and the linebacker grinned, dug his cleats in and got set. Hosea got his head down and his knees up high. That made the grin spread on the linebacker's face—he weighed two hundred and thirty pounds. Only Hosea didn't try running over him; at the last split second he straightened up and gave the linebacker his left leg. When the linebacker shifted in to take it, Hosea pivoted on his right, spinning in a circle like a basketball center playing the key, and while the surprised linebacker went sprawling into the air after a left leg that was no longer there, Hosea shifted back into high and went into the end zone standing up. Son-of-a-bitch!

Blakey looked at the linebacker.

It got even quieter out there. St. Louis in August, hot enough to mangle.

"Boy, I like you," Jabloski said, putting his arm around him. "You play football."

They were out to get him now, hitting him hard and not so clean.

"You're in the wrong place boy. Can't you tell when you ain't wanted?"

"You black son-of-a-bitch. Who in hell you think you are?"

"Go home black boy, 'fore you get your neck broke."

Finally Blakey called it off to prevent a free-for-all. He thought all the tryouts except Jabloski should go home.

St. Louis in August, hot enough to kill.

They dressed in silence. "Jeez, I don't see how he can let you go. You play football," Jabloski told him as they mounted the steps.

Hosea didn't say anything.

"See you," Jabloski said.

Hosea waved and started for the streetcar line.

"Hey you, hey kid?"

Hosea turned around.

"Where the hell you think you're going?"

Now what?

"What's your name?"

Hosea told him.

"Guess you know what you'd be up against in this league? That was just a small sample of it out there."

Hosea didn't say anything.

Blakey puffed on his cigar. "Jesus Christ, you got a great pair of hands, kid. I sure would like to use you. What you think of that?"

Hosea didn't think anything. He was speechless, dumfounded.

Jabloski gave him a lift home and Hosea invited him up for a cup of coffee. That turned out to be a mistake. Mae acted so strange that both Hosea and Jabloski felt uneasy. Finally Jabloski said he had to be running along. Hosea showed him to the door and went outside with him.

"I don't know what's got into Mae," he said. "She ain't never acted like that before."

"Forget it, it don't mean nothing," Jabloski said. "Once you join up, me and you'll set all kind of records in that league, 'cause me and you play football, and ain't that all that matters?"

They shook hands. Hosea went back inside and faced Mae. "What's wrong, puddin? There wasn't no sense in you acting like that. He's a real nice guy."

"I don't want to talk about it," Mae said.

"What you mean? You at least owe me an expla—"

"Hosea, please! I don't want to talk about it."

And she wouldn't.

It was a hell of a note. Here he had spent the whole day knocking himself out for her and his family and they had gotten into their first argument since getting married. In bed, that night, he lay staring at the ceiling for hours.

10

TWO WEEKS WENT by in September, but Blakey did not send for Hosea as he had promised. Finally Mae, tired of him puzzling over it, told him Blakey had come by the house while he was at work, but she had not let him in.

Hosea hit the roof.

Mae wouldn't even give him an explanation.

"You act as bad as one of them Southern crackers," Hosea said.

She refused to say anymore about it. She wouldn't let him make love to her. He didn't want to anyway, not after that. That was too much. Now he couldn't ever expect to hear from Blakey again.

He did though. He got a letter around the end of October. Blakey said they couldn't use him that year, but that they would definitely gamble with him next year, providing this year's team won the championship. He said they would start Hosea at halfback until the public got used to seeing him, then switch him to quarter-back. There was a P.S. in the letter from Jabloski. Jabloski said the championship was in the bag.

There was a cold bite to the autumn wind. Hosea went out into the backyard and gathered a bucket of lumpcoal for the stove. The slick lumps were gummy with cold, coagulated coaldust. Indian summer was gone. It was the time of year when there weren't any stars in the sky.

If they won.

. . . Lord, gonna buy me a pistol, long as I am tall

MAMA WAS FUSSING with Grandpa Argustus and they were moving. Most of the time Mama fussed with Daddy, so today was different.

Moving was fun. There were a lot of boxes and things and Daddy and Grandpa put them in a big truck. They wouldn't let him help though.

"Raymond."

"Huh?"

"Boy, you get yourself out from under your daddy's feet before you get stepped on."

Mama was really mad today. That meant she might not play with him at all.

"Raymond, you hear what I said?"

They moved over where the sidewalks sank down in the middle and cockroaches ran between the cracks. Mama said it was called

Papin Street. They didn't have no grass for grown folks to make you get off of and he had all the dirt he needed to play in!

It was dark down where they lived, and smelled funny. They had a coal bin and a big ole coal furnace. Mama said the furnace would turn red-hot in the wintertime when you put coal in it.

Mama said they didn't live far from L'Ouverture School and he would go there next year.

There were trains by their house. He could stand on the back porch and see them. They huffed and puffed, back and forth, just like the big bad wolf. Sometimes they blew their whistles. Mama said the trains got on her nerves. She didn't like down where they lived either. He did though.

Grandpa gave him a penny when he left, and told him not to tell anybody. Not long after Grandpa left, a man came down the street and got the water to come out of one of those things on the curve. Kids came from everywhere to get in it, gee!

"Raymond!"

"Huh?"

"Don't you move out that yard, you hear me?"

"Uh-huh!"

Shoot, Mama wouldn't never let him do nothing.

They had rocks in their yard. Rocks weren't soft like coal.

He thought Mama would say something about his sitting down in the dirt, but she didn't.

And from the front window, under the porch, Hosea looked out at his son.

"Naw, honey, he's still in the yard."

"It's a wonder. That boy's hardheaded."

"Aw now—"

"He is," Mae said. "He's going to be a problem when he grows up."

"Ain't we all?"

"And if that wasn't bad enough, now I'm going to have another one. Lord knows how we'll manage. We could barely get by on your skimpy check over on Morgan Street, but I rather be down here scuffling than living in a white man's house for free. I'll never forgive Argustus for doing that, not as long as I live."

"He was just trying to help."

"He knows I don't want nothing to do with white folks. He's deceitful too. I wouldn't never have found out if that white man hadn't wanted to move back in."

"That's what I don't understand about you. I ain't exactly crazy 'bout 'em myself, but hell, some of 'em are all right, like Jabloski and Blakey now—"

"What about 'em?"

"Well, Blakey did everything in his power to get me on his team. You got to admit that."

"Did he get you on it?"

"Well, naw, but hell, the depression ain't his fault. Anyhow, he said maybe this year."

"That's what he said last year."

"Well, yeh—"

"And the year before."

"All right, but you ain't helping things none, with that attitude you got."

"You can't blame not making the team on me."

"I ain't trying to, but you sure didn't help my chances none either, acting the way you did when he came to see me."

"So I'm a poor wife and you shouldn't have ever married me in the first place."

"I didn't say that."

"You were thinking it, that's the same thing."

"Well, maybe I was. You could give me a little cooperation around here you know, you don't—"

"And you could take care of your family!"

This was what four years of college and marriage led to?

"You shouldn't have said that."

"I'm sorry."

"I'm doing the best I can."

"I know you are, honey, it's just that, with the new baby coming and everything, and with the money so short, I just stay irritable all the time."

"Yeh, well, maybe the post office will put us back on full time soon."

They had been saying that for years too.

"Oh, I am sorry, Hosea, I really am. I didn't mean—"

But there could be no appeasement. Some things you just didn't say to a man.

. . . Going away, baby, won't be back till fall

WHEN IT RAINED, cockroaches came into the basement. Water did too.

It was a good thing Mama wasn't there.

Cockroaches were fat and black with shiny skin and they popped when you stepped on their backs right. They could crawl up a stick too, if you put it in their way. Rats were more fun, only you didn't see them often. Once he had seen one big as a baby kittycat and it had a large black spot on its side.

A rat's eyes shined in the dark!

A rat had long whiskers and a twitching nose. A rat had long teeth which curved and they didn't look like no Mickey Mouse in the funny papers his daddy read to him on Sundays. Daddy said mice were just like rats, only smaller. Maybe the rat with the black spot wouldn't come back 'cause it was scared. The last time he saw it, he threw some coal at it. He wouldn't do that no more though.

Mama told him the next time she saw him throwing something in the house, she would wear his backside out. Mama hit hard too!

"Raymond?"

"Huh?"

"Put your coat on, we're going to get Mama."

That was Daddy.

Mama hadn't been home for a long time now, and he had spent a lot of time over at Banny's.

Banny told him stories 'bout the slaves and baked him pies in mason jar tops and let him smoke too, just like the grown folks!

He was glad Mama was coming back home though. He missed Mama. Only, when they went to get her, she had a new baby with her and brought her home with them.

"This is your new sister, Helen, Raymond," Mama said. "Your new baby sister, isn't she lovely? Yes, she is. Now Mama's got two little sugar lambs."

Shoot, he didn't want no baby sister.

Mama wouldn't let him touch her and all the grown folks made a big fuss over her, even his Grandpa Argustus. Shoot, he didn't see where she was so hot. She didn't have no hair; she didn't even have no teeth.

"Raymond, what are you over in that corner tuning up about?"

Daddy said a boy never cried.

"And that thumb in your mouth at your age."

But Daddy was always gone somewhere, like now.

"Come here, honey. What they been doing to Mama's baby?"

Daddy said he would grow up to be big and strong like he was someday. Well, when he did, he wouldn't have to cry.

"Aw now, who's been mistreating Mama's sugar lamb? Mama's sweetie pie? Now take that thumb out your mouth. That's Mama's big boy."

And

"Did you finish learning your ABC's?"

"Uh-huh."

"Let Mama see. Show Mama."

He did.

"Now write your name."

He could do that too.

"My, that's Mama's little man. He's going to be just the smartest thing in school, yes he is."

"Mama, I don't want to go to school."

"Aw sure you do now, honey. Now come here and give Mama some sugar."

She hugged him and kissed him.

"Mama, can I play my horn?"

"Honey, now what in the world you want to fool around with that thing for?"

"En-on-ou," he mumbled.

That meant I don't know.

"Oh go ahead. Raymond?"

"Huh?"

"Don't you put nothing in your mouth around here unless Mama says it's all right, not even your horn, you hear?"

"Yes Ma'am."

"And don't you let your sister put nothing in her mouth either. Now bring me that horn before you start playing with it."

Everything was all right again. Only it wasn't. Nobody played with him like before until Grandpa Argustus came to live with them. Grandpa walked with two wooden sticks under his arms and his leg was all in something white and hard like the walls of their house. Grandpa smoked a big ole cigar, but he wouldn't let him take a puff, shoot. Grandpa used a lot of bad words too and Mama got mad. Grandpa had a box you could play music on when you winded it up and a big trumpet he would take out of a black suitcase and shine till it glowed like a Christmas tree, and he told him stories. They weren't the kind of stories his mother used to read him from books, but he liked to listen to them. They were all about a place called Storyville which Grandpa said was down in New Orleans. Mama didn't like Grandpa to tell him stories, but Grandpa did anyway. Then Mama would get mad!

Grandpa said there was a man named Buddy Bolden who used

to blow his horn so loud you could hear him all the way across the Mississippi.

Grandpa said the Mississippi was the biggest river in the whole wide world, gee.

Grandpa could play too! Sometimes he played for Raymond when Mama wasn't home, and he told him not to tell her. He wished Mama could hear Grandpa play. He bet she would like it too. And Grandpa said he was going to show him how to play when he was old enough!

. . . If'n I find me a good gal, won't be back at all

GNATS SWARMED the riverbank. The Mississippi, which looked blue from the distance and brown from a hilltop, was murky gray when you stood on the banks. Mosquitoes were worse than the gnats and you couldn't swing your ax over three or four times without getting drenched in perspiration. The sun cooked the smell of wet weeds hard into your nostrils and made you want to sneeze. Grasshoppers jumped on your pants legs and you had to look out for snakes. The grasshoppers wouldn't leave, unless you knocked them off, and they smeared your clothes with a brown stain they had called tobacco juice when they were kids. The ax handle was wet and slippery in Hosea's blistered hands, and he and Mark cursed as they chopped down the slender saplings lined along the river's edge. When they got up a big enough load, they would strip them down and load up the truck. He wiped the perspiration from his face with a dirty handkerchief, grinding grime into the razor bumps under his chin. He was a man—whump!

And a tree fell.

Didn't he have two arms like anybody else? Arms that could fire a football eighty-five yards down the field or longer if he had to—whump! And legs that could run, hard, bro, and twist and turn and hold a guy up tall so he could walk like a man? And didn't he have a brain that could figure, and plan and think? Didn't he? You damn right—whump!

And the trees fell.

"Clothes props! Two for eight cents! Get your clothes props here!"

They went over Market Street and Morgan and Biddle and down through Johnson, Lasalle, and Hickory, where people barbecued on Saturdays, over metal washtubs with holes knocked in the bottom, propped up off the ground by bricks, and the smell lingered in the air all week long.

"Yea, one nickel'll get you a prop, eight cents'll get you two!"

The old people sat out on the front in wooden chairs, beneath shade trees in the dusty yards.

"Yea, I say eight'll get you two!"

Sunflowers plunged up through the vacant lots, forcing their stalks through the bricks of buildings that had once been there. The kids pulled up the sunflowers, using the roots and the dirt around them for tomahawks and the stalks for spears. They filled paper bags with dirt and threw them out into the street.

Dust bombs.

The kids screamed down the alley barefooted, jumping the coalsheds and pulling out planks from the ancient wooden fences.

"Just one nickel, that's all you need!"

A man took care of his family.

Fat caterpillars webbed the elms and sycamores, and floated down on the passers-by. People burned their nests with kerosene-soaked rags attached to clothes props.

"Will you let me have one on credit, mister? I got nine children in the house and nothing to eat."

So what the hell was a couple of props?

They got hot and tired as hell and they still had to go to work in the post office that night. All over the neighborhood the men sat around idle, playing cards or checkers, or cork ball in the streets.

A woman looked to her man.

All the kids were barefooted. The sun beat down hot, making the summer smells rise—sewers, urine in the gangways, the stuff the dogs left.

Someone hit a police car with a baseball and everybody ran. The police got out, but everybody had gone except the old people sitting on the front and the guys playing cards. The police cursed and got back into the car. The old people watched with tired, hard eyes. The card game went on.

Your voice got hoarse after hollering all afternoon.

The sun was always hot in August. Maybe this year, if things got better? He didn't know if he still had it anymore. He thought he did, but he wasn't sure. Maybe it had been a big joke all the time and they had just been stringing him along? Even so, he was a man, wasn't he? Wasn't he a man?

14

. . . Lord, Lord, C. C. Rider, see what you done done

ON SUNDAY they went to church. The First Baptist church they used to attend was too far away to walk to with a couple of kids so they started going to the little store-front Baptist church around the corner. They took up collection when you first came through the door. The choir didn't have any robes, but they could sing. The preacher was unrestrained and sisters got up and shouted. After they gave the attendance and the financial report they took up collection again. Mae was embarrassed because they had nothing more to put in. Hardly anyone else did either.

"Mama, what's wrong with that lady?"

"Nothing, honey, you keep quiet now."

But there must be something wrong with her, Raymond was sure of that, the way she kept jumping up and down and throwing her arms around.

"Have you got good religion, sisters and brothers?"

"Yes."

"That's the big question facing the world today."

"Sure is now."

"That's right."

"Good religion, that's what the world needs today."

"Amen."

"Yes Lord."

"The kind Daniel had when he went into the lion's den."

"Amen."

"Huh? Now y'all think about that. I said the kind Daniel had when he went into the lion's den."

"Yes Jesus."

"Praise God."

"And if he didn't have it he wouldn't of gone in no lion's den, huh?"

"Naw."

"Uh-uh, naw, he wouldn't of done that."

"And if he didn't ah-have good religion, he wouldn't ah-done got out of no lion's den neither."

"Hallelujah!"

"Glory."

"Now, good religion, that's what I'm talking about."

"Yeh."

"Huh, good religion?"

"Yeh."

The reverend wiped his face and cleared his throat.

"Ain't no other kind worth fooling with?"

"Naw."

"That's the truth."

"Ain't worth wasting your time?"

"Amen."

"And to have good religion you got to have faith?"

"That's the truth now."

"Sure you got to have faith."

"Huh, faith?"

"Yeh."

"Oh-aw-oh fa-aaith now!"

"Yes."

"Hallelujah."

"Preach it brother."

"Fa-aaiith! The kind ah-huh Mo-o-ooses had, when he ah-huh went way down in Egypt land and told old Pha-ai-raoh to let my people go now!"

A sister shouted.

"Yea, I say get your fat, greasy, four hundred years of oppressions hands up off the chosen people and let 'em go now!"

"Amen!"

"Praise God!"

"The Lord moves in mysterious ways!"

"Yea, 'cause the Lord God Jehovah says it's time for the Israelites to move on now."

"Yes."

"And when the Lord God Jehovah says move, what can a man do, but move?"

"Yes, Lord."

"Praise his name."

"I say move! Mo-ooo-ove on down the road now!"

And the sisters shouted.

"And Pharaoh with all his armies couldn't stop 'em."

"Naw."

"That's the truth now."

"Yea, 'cause even the united might of the universe can't stop you if the Lord God Jehovah puts his arm around you and shows you the way."

"Amen."

"So all we need to do if we want to move is get in touch with the Saviour!"

"Yes."

"Praise God."

"Sa-aa-aviour!"

"Preach it."

"And the way you goes about doing that is to get good religion."

"Preach it!"

"Oh praise God!"

"Huh, good religion?"

"Yes."

"Now we don't need be running round begging no President Roosevelt for nothing?"

"Naw."

"We don't need be running round begging Mayor Dickman for nothing?"

"Naw."

" 'Cause they ain't nothing but a man, huh?"

"Yeh."

"Amen."

"A mere ole flesh-and-blood man?"

"Amen."

"Y'all tell me what I say now?"

"Just a man."

"A mere man."

"That's all."

"That's right just a little ole fuddy-duddy man, and when you looking for power to move the universe, you needs to go to the Power Maker."

"Yeh."

"The Generator."

"Oh yes."

"What we needs to do is to get down on our knees and have a little talk with the Saviour."

"Yes."

"The Saviour."

"Amen."

"Preach it brother."

"Oh-oh-ah the Saa-viour na-aow!"

"Yeh."

And the sisters shouted.

The reverend paused and gasped for air.

"And now sisters and brothers have *you* got good religion?"

"Yes, Lord."

"Have you, huh?"

"Yes."

"If you got it, let me hear about it now."

He held up his hand, then he broke out in a singsong voice.

"Tell me, have you-ou got good religion?"

"Certainly, Lord!"

"Oh-aw, have you got good religion?"

"Certainly, Lord!"

"Have you-ooou—"

"Certainly Lord!"

"Yeh-eess!"

"Certainly, certainly, certainly, Lord!"

And they passed the basket around.

15

. . . Yea, C. C. Rider!

EVERY TIME A TRAIN went by, with its whistle blowing, Mae jumped. Hosea knew she didn't like living down in the basement, but hell, neither did he. She didn't have to be so goddamn sensitive.

He started spending a lot of time over on Market Street, playing checkers with Bill and Corky out on the sidewalks. Market Street was full of guys just hanging around. They didn't look each other in the eye much, but he knew what they were thinking—the same thing they had been thinking graduation night when he told them he was going to college, and now here were all three of them loafing on the sidewalk. Corky and Bill had no illusions about college, or making big money. The Cougars said next year, maybe, when things got better, but he knew there would be no next year. It was all over. Cutting trees down in the wintertime would be hell.

One day the police found a whisky still up under the sidewalk in a cave over there on Morgan, where he used to live. The police smashed it and whisky flowed down Market Street like water. Market Street crowded up fast, people popping out of houses from everywhere looking at the stuff flowing down the gutter almost as high as the curb. Some of the guys came running out with fruit jars or any kind of container they could find. They scooped the stuff up with their hats and strained it through a handkerchief or a rag. Corky and Bill got a whole quart jar of the stuff and after it was all over they went back to playing checkers. After a while Corky and Bill got high and started riding him.

"Yeh, college boy, still high and mighty, can't take a little drink with your friends."

"I ain't never took a drink in my life, you know that."

"You ain't never been white in your life neither, but you went running off to college studying business administration like you thought some of them white folks was going put you in they office."

"I could of got a job with a colored firm."

"Why didn't ya?"

"The post office pays more and I got a family."

They laughed and got drunker.

"Bro, if you ain't never had a drink, now's as good a time as any to start."

Maybe they were right.

Corn whisky without a chaser, a red-hot poker searing down his throat and scorching his stomach.

Have you got good religion? I don't know about all that, but I'm sure feeling the spirits. Big joke.

They had to carry him home. He couldn't go to work that night and Mae was more worried about him than the day's pay he would miss.

Once he started drinking he kept it up, and after that there were other women.

16

UNNWWWWANNNnnnnnnnn . . .

*T*HE SOUND that haunted Papin Street.

"I wish they'd do something about those trains running through here driving people crazy with all that noise," Mae complained.

"That's that new streamlined model," Argustus said.

Hosea didn't say anything; he knew better. Hell, why should a man even bother to come home if all his woman was going to do was nag?

"Pattycake, Grandpa?"

"Pattycake, pattycake." This had been going on all morning. "Whew, boy, don't you ever get tired?" Argustus said. "Ask your mama can't you go outside and play."

"No, pattycake."

Argustus pulled Raymond up on his knee. "You know it's downright funny you been born smack dead in the middle of a tornado on the very day Florence Mills died. The good Lord must have some plans in store for you."

"Argustus Anderson, you quit filling that baby's head with all that nonsense."

"Well, you got to admit, yourself, it does seem mighty peculiar," Argustus said. "Ain't that right, boy? What you going to be when you grow up?"

"Storyville."

Argustus laughed. "Boy if you ain't something."

"Raymond, go on outside and play. It's not good for you to sit up under grown folks all day, especially if they're as big a fool as your grandpa."

"Now daughter is that the proper way to talk about your papa?"

... unnn-wwwwWWWWWWWWWNNNNNNNnnnn ...

"Oh, good night," Mae said putting her hands over her ears.

"That all you got to do, sit around and complain about the trains?" Argustus said.

"Is that all you got to do, fill that boy's head with all that nonsense about jazz and blow on that old trumpet when you think nobody's around to know?"

"What?"

"You heard me." Mae turned around. "Raymond, you go on out like I told you now?"

"Yes ma'am."

She turned back to Argustus. "You think I don't know what's going on around here when my back is turned?"

Raymond went out the door.

"Mae honey, I put my horn down seventeen years ago when your maw got killed, you know that."

"But now you're starting back."

Argustus shook his head. "Naw, I ain't never starting back. Far as the world is concerned Argustus Anderson's horn is dead. Every now and then I fool around a little for Raymond, when you ain't here so as not to disturb you."

"Why?"

" 'Cause he begs me to all the time and gets such a kick out of it, that's why. I never seen such a little feller so crazy about music."

"He is not crazy about music! He's too young to know what he likes. Don't think I don't know what you're trying to do. Wilbur wasn't enough to satisfy you. Now you're out to make a jazz musician out of Raymond."

"Naw, I ain't, Mae honey. That boy's just crazy about music. If I didn't tell him the things he wanted to know he'd go find out from somebody else. Anyhow, what you keep jumping down my throat every time I say something about jazz for? I don't understand you, you know that? You growed up right under my horn and still you don't know what it's all about."

"I know it's a lot of sentimental bunk played by a bunch of shiftless people who never had sense enough to grow up."

"It ain't neither no sentimental bunk. Woman, how many times I got to tell you, that's your history coming out of them horns!"

"Instead of trying to play it, you should of been trying to live it. That's what your family was doing while you were up there in Chicago having a good time. We were making history over there in East St. Louis, Illinois."

"You can't leave it be, can you? You got to keep picking at it like it's a big scab or something."

"Let's just forget about it, huh, Argustus?"

"I will not no such thing forget about it. Gal you're holding something back. You've been holding something back all these years; now what is it?"

Mae didn't answer. She backed away from Argustus and went over to the stove and poured herself a cup of coffee.

A train whistle blew and the cup began to jump around in the saucer.

"Mae honey, I asked you a question."

UWWWWWWWWWWWNNNNNNNnnnnnnnnn . . .

The cup of coffee hit the floor, and Hosea jumped up from the chair, where he was studying his post-office scheme, just in time to catch Mae before she did.

Uwwwwnnnnnnnn . . .

And the flames leaped high, roasting the smell of burning flesh against the skyline.

Uwwnnnnnnnnnn . . .

And six thousand drowned in the screams of the pursuing mob, or went down before the bullets of the militia quelling a riot by firing on the victims.

Uwwwwnnnnnnn . . .

And babies were dashed against the sidewalks, and mothers were raped and freight cars went up like torches in the train yard where her mama was ravished and killed by a band of rioters while her young, seven-year-old eyes recorded the scene from between the gigantic shielding wheels of the boxcar under which she was hiding.

Unwwwwwnnnnn . . .

More piercing than lamenting families at two hundred graves.

Unwwwwnnnn . . .

More piercing than Argustus's good-timing trumpet balling them back up there in Chicago.

UNWWWWWWWWWWWWNNNNNNN . . .

Sound from a train taking those lucky folks out of town.

"Mae, what's the matter, honey? It's only a train whistle," Hosea said.

"I'm sorry," Mae said.

"Well, I'll be goddamn," Argustus said looking through the window into the backyard.

They looked to see what Argustus was talking about.

Mae screamed.

There, out in the yard, Raymond was sitting in the dirt, holding Argustus's horn up high as he could and trying his damndest to blow it.

EVERY TIME HE GOT a chance he listened to Argustus's records, but Argustus wouldn't play his horn for him like he used to.

"Raymond! Raymond Douglas!"

"Ma'am?"

"You stop that daydreaming and pay attention."

"Yes ma'am."

Giggles.

"What's three plus three?"

"Six."

Another giggle.

Teacher rapped on the desk with her long wooden pointer. "Carl Logan, what are you sitting back there laughing about? You're just an old gigglebox."

Class laughed and Carl got mad.

"All right, you children, that's enough of that."

When Teacher went out the room chalk and erasers flew everywhere. Mama said she wanted him to be smart and bring home all good grades on his report card. That got you in trouble with guys like Carl.

Carl ran up to the front of the room and looked out into the hall. Then he got the pointer and beat on the desk just like Teacher.

"Y'all shut y'all mouth!" he said.

But class didn't pay him no mind.

"I say for y'all children to hush now!" he said, putting his hands on his hips just like Teacher. They got quiet too. Then ole Jerome had to start his ole giggle and class got noisy again. He ran back to the door and looked out. Wasn't nobody coming. He came back up in front of Teacher's desk and held up his hand. Then he pointed his finger at ole Jerome.

"Hey, boy you," he said.

"Me?" Jerome said.

"Yeh, you. What's you, a school fool?"

Class laughed so he had to beat on the desk. He could make his face do like Teacher's too. "You ain't nothing but a old gigglebox."

Class laughed. Everybody did but Raymond. Carl had everybody all the way up to the third grade scared of him. Carl had a gang.

"Hey ole Raymond Douglas! Ole something overgrown thing!"

Carl laughed, class did too. Somebody threw an eraser that just missed Raymond's head. Mama said he mustn't fight, but that made him mad.

"Don't nobody care 'bout you ole thing," Carl said. "Can't whip nobody."

Jerome laughed just like Woody Woodpecker. Why was Inez looking at him like that? Mama said he mustn't fight.

"All right y'all class, we going read Lesson Four today," Carl said tapping on the desk. He sat down behind the desk in Teacher's chair and started turning pages in the book.

"Let me read, Teacher," Jerome said.

"Naw, let me read, Teacher," Mickey said, holding up his hand.

"Raymond Douglas, boy, you read."

Raymond sat there.

"Raymond."

An ultimatum, join us or else.

Class got real quiet. Then the door flew open and Mr. Purcell walked in.

Uh-oh!

He waved his finger at Carl.

Jerome went Woody Woodpecker and started flapping his arms around when Carl and Mr. Purcell went out the door but class was quiet. Caught at Teacher's desk by the principal, oo-oo-wee!

Teacher came back mad. They didn't get afternoon recess, and she made the room go to the lavatory one row at a time. When Raymond's row went into the latrine he saw his own name scrawled on the wall over the urinal bowl. *Raymond Douglas is a* PUNK, in huge red letters. He didn't know what P-U-N-K meant, but he was sure it must be something bad. He thought of all the bad words Argustus used and picked out the baddest bad one that you could be. That's what he called Carl Logan.

Principal made Carl stay after school for a whole week, and every time he got a chance, all day long, Carl sat across from him and made faces, stuck his fist up to his eye and his nose. That was what he was going to do to Raymond. Next Monday Carl wouldn't have to stay after school.

At three-thirty the bell rang and school was out. Nine hundred children pushing through the doors of L'Ouverture School going home.

"School's out, school's out, Teacher wore her bloomers out!" That's what the big kids sang.

Carl had his gang with him. Jerome, Mickey and Frankie Boy. They walked right by him without saying a word, but that didn't mean nothing.

Some of the kids played leapfrog all the way home, but he didn't do any ripping and running 'cause mama told him he had to take care of his school clothes.

They had patrol boys with pretty white belts holding the traffic back on all the corners. When he got older that's what he would be. He went a block from school. Carl and them were way up ahead. Maybe Carl had changed his mind?

Jerome shoved through the kids crowding the pushwagon where the candyman was.

"Give me one of them penny pickles, mister!"

"You better wait your turn, you ole bad thing," a tall girl in the fourth grade said.

Jerome drew his hand back.

The gang laughed.

"Ha," Carl said. "You scared of a lil ole girl."

"I ain't neither."

Carl and them broke out laughing. Jerome was burning. That's when Raymond came by.

"I bet you even 'fraid of him," Carl said.

"I ain't neither," Jerome said. "Raymond Douglas a punk. Your whole family ain't nothing but a punk. Even your ole mama—"

Wham! Raymond knocked the stars out of him with his lunch box. Jerome tried to get away, but Raymond beat him to the ground and kept on until everybody thought he was going to kill him. Carl, Mickey and Frankie Boy just stood there with their mouths wide open. He was so quiet and smart, they hadn't thought he would fight.

A patrol boy pulled Raymond away and he was crying more than Jerome was. Now he wanted to get away and swing on Carl.

"Aw boy, forget it," Carl laughed. "I ain't mad no more."

Finally the patrol boy let Raymond go.

"Jerome, you ain't nothing. You can't whip do-do," Carl said. "Come on, Raymond. Walk home with us."

"Hah, think you so smart. Got your behind beat," Inez said, skipping by. She grinned at Raymond and then ran away.

That was how it started, he and Carl. Carl was bad. He and his gang played the dozens, talking about people's folks, especially their mamas. Carl didn't care nothing about school. He told lies. He didn't go home until late at night. Sometimes he stole things.

18

"CHILE, YOU MEAN to sit there and tell me you ain't never heard of Nat Turner?"

Raymond shook his head. Helen tugged at his pants leg until she had herself turned around beside him on the floor facing Grandma.

The rocking chair creaked back and forth. Raymond and Helen sat there, their eyes wide open. Story time.

"Now if that don't beat all."

"Who was he, Banny?"

"Who was he? Why chile I 'spect he was just about the baddest darky ever walked this side of God's heaven. He was kin to your cousins on your daddy's side. Why Fred and Hosea look just like him with their big, longheaded selfs," Banny said. Then her voice lowered. "You know they sold your great-great-granddaddy on that auction block down there on Market Street."

Raymond's eyes widened. Helen's did too. The sound of Grandma's voice told her all the words didn't.

"Right out there on Market Street. Now ain't that something?"

"Banny, you quit scaring those children. Why don't you take your old self to bed?"

"Chile, don't you try to run my business."

"Banny, what he do?"

"Aw, chile . . ."

The voice dropped low again. Helen drew up against Raymond as close as she could.

"One of them hot summer nights a long, long, long, Lord, long time ago," Banny said, "Ole Nat Turner decide he done had enough of Mr. Charlie and tired of slavery."

Grandma's voice was shaking. "Wayman." Helen tugged at his pants leg.

"Stop, sister, you pinching me."

"Banny," Bertha said.

"So he sharpened up some knifes and some axes and him and some field hands run out and started chopping off every white head they could find."

"Banny!"

"Well, they sure 'nough did it. Lord knows it's the truth. They ain't spared nothing. Not even them little bitty white folks like your size, Helen honey."

"Wayman?"

"They grabbed them ole white babies like they wadn't nothing and dashed they brains out."

"Wayman." Tugging on his pants leg.

"Banny, now you stop that. Ain't right you should scare them children like that."

But she didn't stop. She told them the whole bloody story, how white folks were still scared twenty years after they caught Nat Turner and hung him and chopped his body up into little pieces and passed what they called the black codes so no darkies could be educated, 'cause Nat Turner could read.

"White folks say darkies is scared," Banny said, "but I can tell you 'bout lots of times when black folks got sick and tired of white folks and done something about it just like Nat Turner."

She would have, too, but Bertha wouldn't let her.

"Mama, can you make grease out of somebody's skin?"

"Why honey, what do you mean?"

"That's what her said."

"That's what *she* said."

"Uh-huh."

"Who?"

"Banny she said the white folks boiled Nat Turner's skin down so they could make some grease."

Mae shifted Helen to another spot against her shoulder. "Honey, why don't you try to walk a little while for Mama?"

She put Helen down on the sidewalk. "Come on now, like Mama's big girl. We'll be to the show in no time."

Ever since the post office had started giving Hosea more hours they had been going to the show on Friday night. They had to cross one of the shaky wooden bridges going over the freight yards in order to get to Market Street. The bridges were poorly illuminated and every time the wind blew they rattled and swayed like they were going to fall down. She had to be careful where they walked, especially the children. The wooden sidewalk had planks missing and some of the places were big enough to fall through.

"Raymond?"

"Ma'am?"

"What else did Banny tell you about Nat Turner?"

"She said he was our kinfolks. She said he looked like Daddy and Grandpa Fred."

"Oh she did, did she?"

"Yes ma'am. She said they sold my great-great-granddaddy on that auction block down on Market Street."

"Oh? Well, she just about talked your earblocks off, didn't she?"

"Yes ma'am. Mama?"

"Yes."

"Were all colored people used to be slaves?"

"You mean here in America? I guess."

"Why?"

"Because that's what they were brought over here from Africa for."

"Why?"

"Because they just were, that's all."

"But, how come, Mama?"

"Because—boy you quit asking so many questions."

"Mama," Helen whined.

"Come on, baby, just a little further. You want to see the movie show, don't you?"

"Uh-huh."

"Then try to walk one more block for Mama."

"Uh-uh."

Mae sighed, and picked her up. It was ten blocks from their house to the movies and they couldn't afford to ride the streetcar. Even in the wintertime they walked, but if the weather was too bad they didn't go. That would just about drive her crazy, not being able to get away from that basement for a whole, solid week.

The wooden steps squeaked as they came off the bridge. Her back ached from carrying Helen. She supposed she should leave her at home until she got old enough to walk like Raymond, but she didn't like the idea of leaving the baby there with Argustus. Look how Raymond had turned out.

19

A MAN CARRYING a horn case, and all dressed up in a suit and a tie, stopped in front of their house. "Hey, boy, what's your name?"

"Raymond."

"Raymond what?"

"Raymond Douglas."

The man picked him up and started swinging around.

"Hey, mister, stop that!"

The man put him back down on the sidewalk. "Where's your mama?"

Raymond stared up at him. What you care? his eyes said.

"She's in the house."

The man punched Raymond on the shoulder. "You're seven years old, ain't ya?"

"Uh-huh, how'd you know?"

"You don't know, do you?"

Raymond shook his head.

"You're a pretty big boy for your age," the man said. "Come on, let's go in the house. I'm your Uncle Wilbur."

Wilbur made Argustus drag out his horn and they played a duet on an old jazz piece Argustus taught him when he was in high school. Raymond got a big kick out of that. Helen did too. Mae was so glad to see Wilbur she didn't say a word.

"You and Uncle Wilbur play some more, Grandpa," Raymond said, but Argustus looked over at Mae and coughed like he had something in his throat. Then he put his horn up.

"Tell you what let's do, let's listen to some records while your mama gets some supper ready," he said. He started selecting some records for the box, then he looked up at Wilbur like he was just seeing him for the first time. "Boy, what in the world you do to your hair?"

"That's a conjugal wave."

"What's the matter, your mama's hair ain't good enough for you?"

"Well, I figured it's been looking like hers long enough and it was about time I got it to look like it took after your side of the family." Wilbur laughed.

"I ain't never wore my hair glued to my scalp like no skullcap," Argustus said. "That was a damn fool thing to do."

"All the musicians are doing it," Wilbur said.

"I don't care who's doing it. It's still a damn fool thing to do. Don't make no kind of sense at all," Argustus said.

Wilbur let it drop. "Hey, Sugar," he said, grabbing Helen and pinching her on the cheek. "You going be my girlfriend?" He kissed her on the cheek. "Ummmmm."

"Boy, you sure ain't changed none. What brings you back to dirty old raggedy St. Louis?"

Wilbur looked at Argustus and frowned. "Remind me to tell you about it sometime," he said.

"You still like skillet bread?" Mae wanted to know.

"Don't I! Hey, where's that husband of yours?"

"Down on Market Street visiting. He'll be home pretty soon though, he's got to go to work tonight. You know we were worried to death about you when we heard about that race riot they had up there."

"Aw, that wasn't nothing like that thing you got caught in in East St. Louis that summer I was visiting down in Louisiana," Wilbur said.

They looked at each other uneasily. Then Mae turned her back on him. "I better watch what I'm doing, I don't want to burn up the skillet bread," she said.

Wilbur cleared his throat. "Yeh," he said. Wrinkles came back on his forehead. Then he held out a record from the stack he was looking through. "Hey, sis, remember this one?"

He flipped it on the record player and started it up.

... *So you met somebody who knocked you right off your fe-eeeeet.*

. . . Goody, goody!

"Lord, I haven't heard that in ages," Mae said.

"Yeh, we used to stomp the ceiling off the joint on that thing, remember?"

Mae smiled. "That was a long, long time ago," she said.

"Aw, ain't been that long."

"A good twelve years if it's been a day," Mae said. "A whole lot of water's passed under the bridge since I've done any of that kind of carrying on."

"Raymond, you ever see your mama dance?"

Raymond shook his head.

"What? You mean to tell me you ain't never seen your mama do the Charleston?"

"How could he?" Mae said. "The Charleston went out before he was born."

"So what? Hey, boy, you didn't know me and your mama used to win all the Charleston contests in East St. Louis, did you?"

Raymond just looked up at him wide-eyed. Uncle Wilbur was trying to play a joke on him. Mama dancing? Not in a million years.

"Hey, he don't believe it. Come on, Mae, let's show him."

"Wilbur Anderson, you must be out of your mind. I haven't even been to a dance since I graduated from college."

"Aw come on." He went over and pulled her away from the stove.

"Wilbur, you quit now."

"Raymond, don't you want to see your mama do the Charleston?"

Raymond looked at him, his eyebrows all knitted up. "Uh-huh."

"Helen?"

"Huh?"

"See, the whole family's behind you," Wilbur said.

Argustus took the needle off the record and started it from the beginning. "Go 'head, it might do you some good."

Her brother hadn't changed at all. As silly as the whole thing was she let him lead her into the steps and the next thing she knew they were off just like old times, elbows flying, legs crossing, then the forward crossover with the double step back, which was their own special invention and the Suzy Que tagged on to boot.

... Hey, hey, hurray and hallelujah ...

Raymond and Helen stood there gaping. This was Mama?

... Aw, yeh, now, you know you had it coming to ya ...

Raymond knew she could smile, even laugh sometimes, but dance? That was beyond comprehension, and there she was, right before his eyes, doing all three at the same time.

... Oh, oh, goody, goody for him ...

... Yea, yea, goody, goody for me ...

"Hey, am I invited?"

"Hosea!"

... And I hope you're satisfied you rascal—

"Hi, puddin" *... You-ooo-uuu ...*

"Hey, Wilbur, when did you get in town?"

"Well, I figure if I'm going to starve to death I might as well be at home." He was grinning when he said it.

Wilbur never did get around to telling them why he left New York. They thought they had pieced it together, figuring the depression was just as hard on musicians as it was on everyone else. They didn't press him about it. He wasn't good company after that first day. He was moody. He would start to talk about something and cut it off right in the middle of a sentence. One by one his suits disappeared down into the pawn shops, and finally his horn. He almost cried like a baby after that. Finally he got on in the post office down there with Hosea early in '36. They rented the whole house when that happened, Hosea and his family moving up on the first floor and Wilbur and Argustus staying down in the basement. Raymond was down in the basement all the time worrying Wilbur until he told him about the things that had happened to him while he was blowing his horn in New York City. Wilbur taught Raymond how to listen so that he could tell who was blowing on a record just by hearing a couple of bars. After a while that kid's ears opened up so wide he could damn near hear as good as Wilbur. That boy was a killer, he had musician stamped all over him no matter what

Mae thought. He didn't tell Raymond everything that had happened to him in New York though. He didn't tell him about Marsha. He left that out, that along with the real reason for leaving New York. Now that he was back in St. Louis, he wondered if he wasn't the biggest fool in the world. Sometimes he thought if he didn't hurry up and find a gig where he could blow his horn he would go stone crazy.

"Hey, boy, you hear what happened to Bessie Smith?" Argustus asked him one morning.

"Naw, what?"

"She was in a car accident down there in Mississippi and bled to death 'cause the white folks wouldn't let her in their hospital," Argustus said.

That didn't make him feel any better.

*A*LL OVER THE neighborhood the streets were deserted.

The streetlights were on and you could hear the crickets chirping if you were outside listening. No one was outside. They were all in their houses crowded around the radio.

The announcer's voice, introducing the fighters, cut across the roar of the crowd. "The—heavyweight—champeen—of the world . . . Jimmy Braddock!"

The roar of the crowd cut out the announcer.

"Who you think's going to win, Uncle Wilbur?"

"Shush."

Forty-five thousand cheering in Chicago Stadium and then the bell went off.

"And there's Louis putting that educated left jab high on the champ's forehead."

"Come on Joe, you can do it," Argustus said.

The champion caught him with another right-hand.

Argustus shook his head.

Round Two and Braddock nailed Louis coming in with a hard right to the jaw. Argustus's eyes blinked. "Take it easy now boy, take it easy."

"Oooh, another hard right to the head as Louis runs away from that annoying left jab."

"Boy, I told you to watch the right. I told you," Argustus said.

"A left, a right."

The crowd screamed.

"Hang on Joe, hang in there," Hosea said.

"You never can tell about this Louis. He keeps that pokerface expression on his face all the time, won't reveal a thing. There's a hard left hook to Louis' nose."

Wilbur slapped the radio with a rolled up newspaper and shook his head. To think he took off from work to hear this.

"Oh, now it's the champ running into a hard, short right cross thrown by Louis. It snaps his head back. The champ moves back from the challenger. Oh, Louis catches him again and there's the bell."

"Anybody want another one?" Wilbur said, getting up to go back to the icebox for another bottle of beer.

"Yeh, bring me one," Argustus said.

"Me too," Hosea said.

Helen begged for some, Raymond did too. Every now and then they got a little sip; not much though, because Mae didn't like it.

Round Three brought the crowd to its feet and also the Douglas household. "That hard left hook bothered him. Yes, Louis fires a right high on his forehead. He's hurt, he's hurt. Ladies and gentlemen the champ's in trouble!"

"That's it. What'd I tell you? I told you he'd do it!"

"Be quiet, Argustus, how you expect people to hear?" Mae said.

After that the champ stayed in trouble.

Round Five, "Braddock's hanging on."

"Kill that mother, Joe. Knock his D string loose," Wilbur said.

All over the country they were saying it. "Kill that mother, Joe. Show 'em we just as good as they are."

It was the beginning of a new idol, more powerful than anything that ever existed before, more popular even than Florence Mills. Joe Louis, a big, slow-drawling man from the Georgia cotton fields, who could hardly read or write, and who even had trouble talking, but could deliver the message fine. Joe Louis, the new heavyweight champion of the world. That meant he could lick any man living.

They poured out of the tenements to celebrate it, the sharecropper shacks, the ghettos.

In St. Louis the neighborhoods came alive again. Raymond, Carl and Jerome gave Papin Street a fit. All the kids were out in the streets beating on washboards, and tubs and tin cans; anything they could get their hands on. Raymond led the parade, in his block, blowing on Argustus's trumpet, which he had sneaked out of the house after getting Helen to promise not to tell. They ran up and down celebrating like that for hours, then Carl thought up better things to do. So they went out in the alley and turned over all the garbage cans. Next they took six of them and stacked them up on top of each other right in the middle of the streetcar tracks. Then Carl broke a couple of lamppost lights and everybody ran home.

It didn't stop after that night. Joe Louis was something better than Jesse Owens who went over there and outperformed all those Hitler supermen, and when his champion, Max Schmeling, came over here and lasted one round, Joe Louis could do no wrong. The master race had been dumped flat on the seat of its can and a black fist had done it.

The weekly Negro newspapers tried to stem it off, warning that Joe Louis was human and had to lose sometime, just like any other man, but they all knew that was a lie. Joe Louis couldn't lose. Joe was their self-respect.

21

. . . my mama done tole me, when I was in knee pants . . .

BANNY SAID THE MOON turned orange when autumn came because its face kept getting slapped with a cold breeze. Banny said if you made a wish on a night when you could cast your shadow by moonlight it was sure to come true. He didn't believe that.

He was a child of the wind, playing all the wind games. He and Carl and Mickey and Frankie Boy and Jerome. They ruled the fourth grade. They ruled their part of the yard and nobody messed with them either. They ripped back and forth, during the recess periods, flopping boys down and daring them to get mad, corking each other on the arms until their arms ached, thumping the heads of the boys who had their hair cut real close to the scalp. And after school there was football on the vacant lots, tramping the sunflowers and the weeds down, and there were tin cans beneath your feet just like horseshoes once you got your shoes fitted into the center which had been caved in with a brick.

He went like the wind, hurrying through school days, brusque mannered, impervious, and fickle, all in the same day, laughing a high, gay laugh. And when school was over he and his friends hurried through the school gates to wade in the crackling leaves drying in the gutters. Fall was a dying season and he was alive. The wind batwinged the Halloween moon and brought the witches out. The wind scattered the autumn smells and when it tired of that the wind laughed, a dying turkey's laugh, and brushed the sun-shadowed landscape with dull-bright colors. He went with the wind, growing cold with the wind, growing old with the wind and not knowing why.

And better than anything else he liked being down in the basement with Argustus and Wilbur. Every week Wilbur let him shine his trumpet and listen to him practice. He was always telling him to go someplace and play, but Raymond knew his uncle better than to pay it any mind.

"Boy, when you grow up you be something smart like a school-teacher, or a preacher, you hear? You let yourself get in a groove behind one of these horns and it'll drive you stone cold out of your mind."

Argustus wasn't saying much these days. He could see hunger in the boy's eyes, a racial hunger that glistened every time Raymond looked at a horn.

One evening Hosea came in with a newspaper all spread out in front of him. "Get a load of this," he said, shoving it in front of Wilbur's nose.

"Elmer, Jolting, Jabo, Jabloski, local boy, who became big-time star in professional football, retires after a ten-year career. So what?"

"Well, yeh, but read right there, where he's talking 'bout the greatest players he's ever seen at each position."

"Huh, oh yeh," Wilbur said.

"You see it, Argustus?"

"See what?"

"Right there where it says the greatest player he ever saw at quarterback never got a chance to play pro ball."

"Yeh, I see it. So what?"

"He was talking about me," Hosea said. "Come on, Raymond. It's time you went to work and learned something."

"What'd you make out of that?" Wilbur said as they went out the door.

Argustus shrugged.

Raymond had good co-ordination. In six weeks' time Hosea had taught him how to make a fool of everybody his size in the neighborhood with a football. Everybody except Carl. But he and Carl always played on the same team, which meant the other kids were always up against it.

One evening, just before the first snow of the season, Hosea stopped by on the corner lot, to get a line on how his kid was coming along. What he saw made his eyes pop.

There was Raymond taking the handoff from center and fading for the sidelines like a midget pro. He danced around a kid rushing in, then planted his feet and threw like Hosea had taught him, putting his shoulder and all his weight behind it. The ball went a good twenty-five yards and a dark, husky kid called Carl caught it. That Carl was a hell of an athlete already, Hosea could see that. When those two got to high school, look out. He was almost late to work watching them. They had stopped him. They wouldn't stop his son.

SOME YEARS it snowed a lot. Like the winter of '38 when Banny died. Bertha went around telling everyone Banny was eighty years old so it was about time she died, but at the funeral she cried all through the services.

They held the wake and funeral down at Mount Sinai, the big Baptist church on Leffingwell and Laclede where all the Douglases used to go at one time or other. Banny had gone to church every night there for as long as most folks could remember and when they sang that song . . .

> Wade in the water, children . . .
> God's gonna trouble the water . . .

They sang it like they really meant it, but Raymond didn't like the way the preacher kept talking about Banny like he knew all about her, and every good thing she ever did, when he knew he didn't. They stayed in church a long time and snow piled against the windows.

There was nothing left of Banny but a dressed up, ash-gray body and a stiff face set in death-locked lines. Helen cried and Mama made her blow her nose. Then Mama blew her own nose.

By the time the Douglases finally left church the snow was settling like white dust pockmarked with soot from the smoky air. By morning six inches of snow had fallen and you couldn't tell where the street curbs ended and the streets began.

It took three hours to get out to the graveyard.

It took an hour and a half to get the grave ready and decide it was decent to drop her in.

It took two minutes to lower her down.

Then everybody but the grave fillers went home.

Right after that Wilbur quit the post office for a three nights a week gig where he was lucky to make room and board. Mae thought that was awful. Raymond did too, because his uncle didn't spend much time with him anymore. He was always telling Raymond he was busy. One time he came down and there was a woman in Uncle Wilbur's bed. After that he had to knock. Raymond didn't know what to think. Then came the day that ended everything. He was helping Uncle Wilbur shovel snow off the sidewalk in front of their house, and Uncle Wilbur turned and said, "Look, pal—see there's this ofay band I got this offer with. What I mean is I guess I got to put this town down. Hey, don't look like that. I'll be back to see you."

"You won't neither. You ain't gone never come back."

"Yes I will, I promise."

"You promised we'd be pals and you'd stay and show me all about music."

"Well, I did. I didn't mean forever. Aw, look pal, try to understand. You can't expect me to stay here now that I got this offer to play all over the country with this white band. This is a big-time outfit, the first chance I ever had to make some real dough. Ernie Fergen's a real—"

But there was no reasoning with a ten-year-old kid.

"Aw look, Raymond. Come on downstairs, I got a present for you."

"I don't want it."

"Aw come on."

It was all wrong.

"What's the matter, Raymond? Don't you like your present?"

His uncle hadn't bought him a horn, he had bought him a sled.

"Hey, now wait a minute, sport. Ain't nothing to cry about." He knew what the trouble was, but what the hell, Argustus had told him about Mae. So he packed up in a hurry and went upstairs to tell everybody goodbye. Everybody but Raymond, Raymond wouldn't hear of it. He just stood there betrayed.

First Banny, then his Uncle Wilbur. For years that's what snow reminded him of.

"Yeh, you black and yo mama."

"You dodo head. I'ma beat your butt."

"Aw nigger, you ain't gone do nothing. Dodo on you and yo mama too."

Uh-oh!

"Carl Logan, what's wrong with you? You better sit down back there."

"Well shoot, Miss Austin, he said—"

"I don't care what he said. You keep your little fresh self in your seat."

"I'ma stomp a corn on his head."

"Aw, nigger, you don't scare nobody."

"Carl Logan, did you hear what I said?"

"Well shoot, Miss Austin. He said You black and yo mama."

"Does he know your mother?"

"No'm."

"Well, how can he talk about something he doesn't know anything about?"

"Well, he said You black—"

"I don't see why you should get so excited about him saying that? Both of you are the same color."

"Score!"

"Score!"

"Children!"

"Oo-oo, Teacher scored!"

"I know one thing. I'm going to keep the whole class after school if you don't start acting like you've got some sense."

Miss Austin was a huge woman, in her early thirties, weighing close to two hundred pounds. She hit like a man, and when she said something she usually meant it. You didn't go up against Miss Austin. The class got quiet. The boys didn't even gesture at each other, but there would be a fight outside before the day was over, sure as the sun would rise. James had come to school that first day and started something with Carl because everybody told him he was the baddest thing there. James was two years older than most of the class, but he wasn't any bigger than Carl. He was dirty and there were holes in the knees of his overalls. His socks showed through the scuffed top of his shoes and he wore a big army sweater instead of an overcoat. Somebody said he was from Mississippi, but nobody had nerve enough to say it to his face, because of another rumor that was out. They said James was carrying a knife.

It happened during the second recess, when all the boys in the fifth grade were sliding on frozen puddles, on the boys' side of the schoolyard. Carl and James stood, a few feet apart, looking at each other. Most of the time the class pushed the two guys together if they were slow in getting the fight started, but with Carl and James they didn't dare. Carl just stood there, his leather cap jammed over the bridge of his nose, rubbing his leather gloves together, diamond designed, long socks tucked in straight under his corduroy knickers, husky shoulders bunched up under a warm, cheap mackinaw, eyes already set hard in a strong, young, dark face. The way he stared at James's clothing made the class laugh.

James got mad. "Yeh, nigger, that's all you better do, just look."

Carl threw his shoulder like he was going to hit him.

James jumped back. "Yeh, you ole liver-lipped black spasm, I wish you would." He put his hand in his pocket.

Carl punched at him for real then, but not before James got his hand out of his pocket. The class gasped. James really did carry a knife; not just a little pocketknife either, like a lot of the boys carried, but a sure 'nough for real spring bouncer where the blade shot out when you pressed a button on the handle. But Carl had already hit him and it was too late to stop now. So he hit him again while James had the knife drawn back and the knife flew out of his hand. James turned and ran for the knife, but Jerome kicked it out of his way and Frankie Boy stepped on it. James looked at Jerome, Frankie Boy, Raymond, and Mickey. All of them were looking at him hard-eyed. Bright eyes cutting in dark faces. Carl beat hell out of James. He kicked him too, every time he knocked him down, and once he caught him on the left side of his head closing the eye.

They suspended Carl from school for a whole week.

"That nigger's lobo," James said, meaning Carl was what the cowboys called loco, but the name stuck. From that day on Carl was known as Lobo.

They sent James to Bellefontaine Farm Reform School, because of the knife. James stayed there a whole year and when he got out they transferred him to Raymond Crow elementary school. The word came down James was head of the Compton Hill Midgets and Lobo better watch out. They put rocks in snowballs and threw at the streetcars, running down the brick alleys screaming at the top of their voices. They flopped down four and five on top of each other on the same sled. They bought cigarettes, for a penny apiece, at the corner grocery stores and smoked them out back in the coalsheds. They made blocks out of snow with empty tin cans and built igloos. They shoved over snowmen the girls made, and dared them to tell. They caught the Lone Ranger and Tom Mix on the radio and they went out front with their fathers and shoveled the lump coal, left in a pile in front of their houses by coal trucks, into a wheelbarrow so that it could be dumped through the basement windows. That's what winter was all about.

FOREVER WAS A sunny day when the sky was cloudy like milk and the dirt on the ground felt spongy and smelled like dogs.

Forever was shooting marbles in Jerome's back yard, on Chouteau Avenue, where grayish-green water bubbled into muddy puddles from the busted toilet pipe in the middle of the yard, and roaches ran over the back wooden porches from the garbage and trash where the rats played in the eight-family flats.

Forever was walking the ragged wooden fences and jumping from roof to roof on the sagging coalsheds.

Forever was junk-hunting in the alleys for the pennies the grocery stores paid for bottles and running from the police.

Forever was taking a bath in a metal washtub and heating cold water on a potbellied coal-burning stove.

Forever was throwing rocks and tin cans at the kids across the alley and catching grasshoppers and pulling lights out the tails of fireflies.

Forever was spinning tops and skating in the streets and stealing pears from the caterpillared pear trees.

Then came the day when forever stopped. A new kid named Tack moved into the neighborhood. Tack said the back yard and the gangways and the hallways in the house stank. Tack said the thousand, billion, zillion ole fat black horseflies with green heads and red noses, in Jerome's yard, spread filth and disease around.

Tack ought to know. Tack was the son of a doctor who they said was in jail 'cause he got rid of a baby for some dame who got knocked up. Tack was the only kid in their class who could wear good clothes to school. Tack said their hair was nappy and wore his own in long curly bangs slicked back in hard waves underneath Murray's pomade. Tack got mad at Inez 'cause she got better grades than he did in school and sometimes he fell out with Raymond for the same reason. The only reason Tack didn't get his butt beat every day was because he was a friend of Raymond's. He came over to Raymond's house all the time and listened to him play his horn. Tack had a piano at home and sometimes his mama would let him bring Raymond over and Tack would play while he blew his horn. Tack could really play that piano, but his mother wouldn't let him play jazz so Raymond didn't have much fun playing over there. Tack had a chemistry set and a train and he let Raymond play with them. Tack told Raymond about schools where kids tried to learn something and the teacher didn't snatch guys back into the cloakroom and wear their hides out like what happened to Jerome and Frankie Boy and even Lobo sometimes, and where guys didn't stink up the basement by peeing all over the wall when nobody was around, or draw nasty pictures of guys and dames doing things and write bad words all over everywhere with red crayola. Lobo called Tack a old fat-butt sissy. Lobo told Tack all he knowed how to do was sit around the house like an old woman on his fat old rusty-dusty. Tack showed up next day in Jerome's back yard, with a pocketful of marbles for the marble game.

"You better stay out, Tack," Raymond told him. "We playing for keeps."

"I know it," Tack said.

"Aw, let that ole liver-lip fool play if he wants to," Lobo said.

Jerome gave Tack his Woody Woodpecker laugh. Jerome could peel from ten feet out and hit and stick. Jerome could lag. Jerome could roll. There wasn't anything Jerome couldn't do with a steely in a big ring.

Tack was better.

They couldn't get over it. Tack was better!

Tack could peel and knock more marbles out the ring with his shooter than Jerome could with his steely!

Lobo got mad and hobbled all of Tack's marbles that were in the ring.

"Hey, you gimme them back," Tack said rushing toward Lobo.

Lobo turned his back on him. "Gawn boy 'fore y'all get hurt," he said.

"Gimme," Tack said grabbing Lobo by the arm.

Lobo hit him a backhanded blow with the side of his arm. "I said gawn now." Lobo looked around for all to see who was still king of this neighborhood.

Tears started sneaking down Tack's thin cheeks.

Lobo started throwing Tack's marbles as far as he could over the coalshed, one by one, trying to reach the rooftop of the flats on the other side of the alley.

Tack ran in as though he would stop him.

Lobo frowned and hunched down into a crouch with his fists balled up. "Boy, you better go on home 'fore I beat yo butt," he said.

Tack stopped and looked at him.

Lobo smiled and threw Tack's shooter farther than any of the other marbles. Tack's shooter sparkled like a green jewel arching high as a rooftop in the sunlight.

Tack ran off sounding like a fire siren. Everyone started laughing, except Raymond. What'd he do that for?

"Boy, what's wrong with you?" Jerome wanted to know.

Lobo looked him over with his cold brown eyes. "Aw forget it," Lobo said. "That punk ain't got no business over here shooting marbles with us noway."

Lobo got rid of the rest of Tack's marbles.

All over the alley dogs barked at shiny glass balls gliding down into their back yards in glittering arches.

25

. . . my mamma done tole me, son . . .

THEN A YEAR went by and he knew why Lobo looked at girls
like that; he knew. He looked too, not like Lobo, straight at them
so they could see, but when he thought they weren't paying him
any attention that was when he looked, and at night when he was
in bed he did things he was ashamed of.

There were a lot of girls in the neighborhood and he and Lobo
started fooling around with Marie, and Elmira, and Joanna, and
Lorraine Jordan. They'd sit on each other's steps, the whole neighborhood would, and sing songs, or they played cops and robbers,
but the favorite game was highspy. That was how you got a girl
alone with you in the dark. He didn't never do nothing though
because he didn't know how to go about it and anyway the Bible
said . . .

Lobo did though, at least he said he did and Raymond believed
him because Lobo and Elmira used to hide together all the time
and sometimes they would end up finishing the game without them.

They played post office too. You got to kiss a girl that way if
the letter was delivered to you. He was anxious. He was eager. He
throbbed with an excess of energy. He had a man's hunger in a
boy's body and it never gave him a minute's rest. Girls teased him
with their tight-fitting skirts, switching by with blouses pulled down
tight over their small young breasts, and they found excuses for
crossing their legs slowly so he could imagine what he thought he
was seeing. The girls teased all the boys in the neighborhood and
pretended not to know what they were doing.

One day some older guys came by on the sidewalk while they

were sitting on Lorraine Jordan's porchsteps and the long, tall dark one everyone called Snake called to Lobo.

Lobo shrugged and went on down.

"We starting the Hawks," Snake said.

"Yeh, and we gone wear blue sweaters with white Hawks on the back," Fatblack said.

"Yeh, we gone be the toughest thing in town, show him, Weasel," Snake said, nudging a short, narrow-faced guy with hair greased down over his head.

Weasel pulled a twenty-one pistol out from behind his belt and shoved it in front of Lobo's face.

"See that," Snake said. "We got a whole case of 'em."

"Yeh, we hung that train yard over there on Chouteau for 'em," Fatblack said.

"Yeh, little bro, when we get through with the Turks and Compton Hill, nobody won't even remember 'em ever being around," Weasel said.

"Yeh," Fatblack laughed, "and if them chickenshit sugarhills starts to mess around they gone be preaching they own funeral services."

"We need some midgets, you wanna be president?"

"Well, uh—yeh Snake, I guess so," Lobo said.

"Okay then, tell all your boys. Here," Snake said, handing him the pistol. "This is yourn."

"Tell him the signal, Fatblack," Weasel said.

"Ee-oo-weeth. Ee-oo-weeth! That's it," Fatblack said.

After they had gone Lobo strutted before the neighborhood like he owned the world. "Hey Raymond, we midgets now. Boy, just wait til Jerome and Frankie Boy and them find out. Ee-oo-weeth. Ee-oo-weeth!"

He hid the pistol in the cloakroom at school where they had their spring bouncer knives and Sneaky Pete wine.

All of Raymond's friends except Tack were in it. They didn't want nothing to do with nobody acting like Tack.

"Boy, that Tack," Lobo would say shaking his head. "Ewe, he sho is square."

Raymond didn't want to have anything to do with the whole business, but how could you tell that to a guy like Lobo when you were living in a neighborhood like Papin Street and were only twelve years old?

. . . a woman's a two face, a worrisome thing . . .

BACK IN NEW YORK and glad to be there. Back in the big city and all Wilbur could think of was Marsha Perkins and a chance to blow man, down in a dark, dank basement somewhere, to a pigs' feet and beer crowd, the way he used to in Jack the Bear's way back there a long time ago.

She showed at his dressing room the third night in town. One thing about New York, they might not let your folks out front in the audience, but they could sure come backstage to see you. Big deal.

Marsha had put a on a good ten pounds. It hadn't hurt her appearance.

He had left in '35 because he couldn't get a gig; any kind of a gig. Marsha had wanted to get married anyway. Now he was the one, but when he told her she started to bawl and wouldn't come in on the conversation. Now wasn't that the lick?

He went out and bought her a $750 engagement and wedding ring set. That called for more tears. She took the rings, but wouldn't wear them. Man, now that was the lick!

Then, almost before he knew it, their three-week run at the Congo was over and he had to leave town.

"I don't even know how to get in touch with you again," he said.

"Wilbur, you know how I feel about you. I don't 'spect that's gone ever change, but you can't get in touch with me."

"What you mean, Pretty? Why not?"

She tried clowning around and he grabbed her, so angry he could have choked her.

They wound up making love down on the hotel room floor.

What she told him later didn't make him feel any better. "I prayed to the Lord for ten years to marry you, Wilbur," she said.

A tear got away from her eye.

She went into her bag, got out a wedding band which wasn't his, and slipped it on her finger. "Honey, I'm already married." Her small voice trailed off as she went out the door. "I even got two kids," she said.

Now that was the lick, the lick that laid poor Dick out deader than a doornail and that wasn't no lie.

IT WAS THE Fourth of July and Mama said he could go to Forest Park with Lobo and them.

They wore tennis shoes, white T shirts, and levis. They had a pocketful of firecrackers and they hid in gangways and threw them out at passing cars. That was a lot of fun when somebody got mad enough to stop. Then they'd run through the gangways laughing and pushing each other out of their way.

They wore white handkerchiefs, tied around their heads sheik style. That meant you were a gang. If you wore one around your fist it meant you were out looking for trouble.

They sneaked in the back door of the streetcar without paying and the streetcar conductor acted like he didn't see them. The car was full of people with picnic baskets going out to Forest Park to celebrate.

Somebody threw a firecracker out the window at an old ragman shoving a pushcart down Laclede Avenue.

It exploded and the old man jumped and turned loose the handle of the pushcart. The pushcart dumped the carefully selected trash all over the middle of the street.

The Compton Hill Juniors got on the streetcar down around the big vacant lot on Grand Avenue. The Compton Hills wore blue work handkerchiefs on their heads. They started joaning with the Hawk Midgets. That made the streetcar kind of noisy. One of the Compton Hills started rolling a big pair of white dice down the middle of the aisle. Most of the young dames on the streetcar were wearing shorts. They teased the guys when their parents weren't looking.

There were police hanging round out at the end of the carline, where the streetcar turned around across from Forest Park, so they had to play it cool. Once they got out in the park, though, they really let go. The park was a good place to find dames. Sometimes they had gang fights out there.

They ran into some dames down by the boathouse. It was their classmates Inez Claybanks, Joanna Friar, and Juanita Paine.

Inez had a baby face with big eyes and a wide mouth, but her body looked as grown-up as a movie star's. Inez was soft all over, at least he imagined she was, and every time she looked at him it made him want to do things. They said she was fooling around with some guy in high school, but that didn't mean nothing; they were always saying something about her, 'cause she'd slug any boy in their class that laid a hand on her. There was another thing that kept the boys away from Inez. She was the smartest thing in class. Once she told him she would be his girlfriend, but that was a long time ago when he didn't care nothing about dames and besides she had been trying to beat him out of some of his crayola. Dames were always trying to beat guys out of something.

Lobo and them tricked him into staying with Inez while they went off in the woods with Juanita and Joanna. Maybe this was his lucky day.

They went for a walk themselves and they found a little clearing on the other side of the pavilion where they could stretch out. They didn't talk about nothing much. He didn't know how to talk to girls.

After a while Inez got careless and stopped smoothing her skirt down.

Then they got to wrestling and after a while she told him to get up.

She was soft all over!

All over the park you could hear firecrackers explode.

He caught one leg of her underwear and jerked it to the side.

It was his lucky day.

Inez and Raymond graduated at the head of their class. Raymond's mother was proud of him.

Inez told him she was getting married to some guy who was a freshman in college.

"Ooo, rock me mamo in yo big brass bed," Eddie "Cleanhead" Vinson sang on the Y circus stage down at Kiel Auditorium. "Ooo, squeeze me til my face turn chee-aar-reee red."

28

WILBUR ANDERSON had arrived. He was the real King in the music circles these days. There was no denying him. He became a legend before his thirty-fourth birthday and the giant god money rolled in. Ernie Fergen's aggregation made the biggest splash of any band that ever hit L.A. and that's when things really got bad for Wilbur.

One night he missed a high C during the second show and the next thing he knew he began to lose track of time. One day he came to himself out on Central Avenue waving prostitutes off the streets with ten-dollar bills. He found out he had gone through a whole week's bank roll that way. Then the Japs knocked hell out of Pearl Harbor and he got drafted.

They made him a foot-soldiering yardbird all the way; wouldn't let him in Special Service, said he wasn't a bonafide entertainer, and here he had won the UpSwing jazz poll two years in a row.

He made all the K.P. sets. He piled up potatoes humming a tune that kept popping up in his head. Each chance he got he worked on that tune until he had the blues pattern flowing smoothly as spontaneous changes in a jam session solo. That tune got real high up on the hit parade charts. It made him a lot of dough. Some of it he sent home to Argustus and Mae. He named that tune "Marsha."

. . . that leads you to sing the blues in the night . . .

THE HAWKS SAID they'd better not catch anybody out on the streets after ten o'clock at night.

Ee-oo-weeth . . . Ee-oo-weeth!

It all started when Cooty got stabbed for visiting a girl on Clark Avenue, right across from Mama Rosa's. It was his first gang war and he never forgot it; the Hawk Seniors, Juniors, and Midgets against the Turks and the Compton Hills.

Lobo tried to burn somebody that night. Snake and Fatblack did too, but it was too dark and they couldn't get a good look at who they were shooting at.

Women with nothing on but their panties crowded the windows at Mama Rosa's, to see what was going on. Somebody called the police, but they never bothered to show up. In the meantime the Hawks caught up with a Turk and gave him to the midgets to work over.

Lobo and them socked him out, they really laid him open. Raymond was in on it too, he hit him once, just once, good and hard though. You had to hit 'em at least once; otherwise your own guys would jump on you.

After the fight Snake, Weasel, and Fatblack went into Mama Rosa's. They took Lobo in with them.

After that night the running really started. The ducking, dodging and fear started. They had to cross the Compton bridge, which was deep in Compton Hill territory to get to Vashon High School; so they'd all meet in the mornings and walk the bridge together. The same thing happened at three o'clock.

Then Raymond joined the school band. That meant he had an *A* period class at eight o'clock in the morning when the band practiced.

That meant he had to cross the bridge all by himself.

As it turned out he had nothing to worry about. The Turks and Compton Hills didn't get up that time of morning.

It was right along through then that joyriding became the thing. Lobo and them spent their evenings finding unlocked cars and jumping the ignitions with cigarette tinfoil stuck under the starter.

They went joyriding every night. Sometimes they'd pick up some chick like Lorraine or some other dame that was easy. One day Lobo and them got it in their heads they wanted to go to Canada. He told them he couldn't go because he would miss band practice.

. . . miss band practice?

Here they were, ready to take off for Canada and then to New York and Mexico maybe . . . band practice?

. . . damn, Raymond, you sure getting to be a square.

They called him chicken.

They got caught in Indiana after Jerome pulled off from a filling station without paying for a tank of gas.

They got put in a detention home for six months and he went to see them every Sunday. After that Lobo and them were back on the streets with a bigger reputation than ever.

Then Mama found out about him being in the band. Helen snitched on him.

"Ole tattletale," he told his sister, "I'ma beat your butt."

Mama beat his with an ironing cord.

He said he should have gone off with Lobo and them in that stolen car.

Mama slapped his face good and hard.

Uncle Wilbur sent them a letter with a whole lot of money in it!

Mama started to send it back, 'cause Uncle Wilbur also sent him a trumpet and told Mama if she wanted to keep the money she'd have to let him play it.

In all his dreams at night nipples of bare-breasted women rested on Mama Rosa's window sills.

Night after night Mae thought about it. For a good half year she turned it over in her mind. Then one day, during the last part of '42, they went house hunting. They decided on a two-story residence out west on Cora Avenue away from all the riffraff. They would have to wait at least another four or five months before the owners could move out. That was all right with them. She lived the rest of the year out in fear, jumping at the sound of each passing train whistle, and the wild shadows of her own imagination.

Part Two

So What?

1

. . . Everyday, everyday I have the blues . . .

NO MATTER WHERE he practiced, in their new house, Mama complained.

He tried his own room; Mama complained.

He tried his sister's room; Mama complained.

He went all the way up to Argustus's attic apartment; still Mama didn't like it.

The second floor was rented out to roomers so he couldn't practice there, and the living room, dining room, and kitchen were out of the question.

She even kept him out of the basement, so gee whiz, what was he supposed to do, practice in the bathroom? Shoot, Mama acted like the worst crime in the world was having to listen to him play his horn. He wasn't *that* bad. In fact Mr. Carter, the band director down at Vashon, told him he had a lot of talent. Even Uncle Wilbur admitted he learned fast and Argustus said he would do in a push. Yeh, well, just wait, one of these days he'd be grown and then he'd show them all.

. . . Everyday, ev'ryday I got the blues . . .

THEN HE HAPPENED to go back downtown to spend a little time with Lobo. What'd he do that for? A police car pulled around the corner they were standing on and old Sergeant Holt got out.

"What you boys doing hanging on this corner this time of night?" the sergeant wanted to know.

"Nothing."

That was the wrong answer.

The sergeant made them spread their hands out and push back from the wall of the building on the corner, while another cop went through their pockets.

"They're clean, Sarge."

"It's a good thing for you you are," the sergeant said. "If I ever catch you young punks with anything on you I'll slap you into the middle of next week, you get me?"

They didn't answer.

"Hey fella, I'm talking to you!"

Still no answer.

"What's wrong, boy, you don't hear so good?" the sergeant said, looking at Lobo.

"Yeh," Lobo said. "I hear all right."

"Well, keep your big mouth shut till I ask you something then. I was talking to this boy here."

"Well," Raymond said, "I—"

"Shut the hell up. I'm still talking to little fart here. You understand me, boy?"

Lobo didn't say anything. Lobo didn't play getting called out of his name.

102

The sergeant called Lobo a lot of other names.

"Sergeant, my name is Carl Logan," Lobo said.

"Aw sho 'nough now. Well tell me something you little fart. Do you piss blue ink?"

"Naw."

"Well, you should you little bastard. You're black enough."

WHAM! The sergeant's hand exploded against Lobo's head.

"Now get your little black ass home."

Lobo stood there staring at the sergeant.

Raymond pulled him away. "Come on, Lobo," he said.

WHAM! The sergeant's hand exploded against Raymond's head.

"Boy, who the hell told you you could go somewhere?"

Lobo spat, out the side of his mouth, on the sidewalk. "Paddy bastard," he said.

The sergeant and Lobo locked eyes.

"Boy, you're so bad you should be over there fighting the Japs," the sergeant said. "Now you and your pal get your ass over there in that squad car."

On the way to the police station the sergeant explained the situation to his partner. "Yeh, rookie," he said. "Down here you're just a white face in a black world and don't you ever forget it. The only thing that'll keep them from doing you in is fear, pure and simple fear."

He poked Raymond in the ribs with his nightstick. "Ain't that right, boy?"

3

EVERYBODY IN HIS family was down on him, even Daddy, even Argustus, everybody except Helen and she didn't count. Shoot, how was he to know they were going to lock him and Lobo up and make their folks come down and get them?

The only time he managed to get off the porch, for three whole weeks, was when he went over on Garfield and played tag football with the guys a few hours each day.

Jimmy was the fastest thing on Sumner's track team and Raymond became a big thing around the neighborhood by making a fool of him with a football. One time Raymond faked Jimmy all the way up on top of the hood of a parked car. All the guys got a bang out of that.

Jimmy's brother Freck told Raymond he should make first string on Sumner's varsity.

Jimmy said, "Yeh, if he ain't scared of getting hurt."

Teacher didn't say anything. He didn't fool around with sports. Teacher was the cool one in the neighborhood whose mother let him wear a full-cut zoot suit and who was better at fronting people off than anybody Raymond had ever met before. His real name was Bruce Thomas, but they called him Teacher because he was always telling somebody something they didn't know. Teacher claimed Lobo was his cousin.

The whole summer was turning out to be a drag. Except for practicing football out in the backyard, with Daddy before he went to work, and going over on Garfield, he didn't have anything to do. Then it was time for the annual block dance, over in the Cote Brilliante schoolyard, and Helen wanted to go. Mama said he had to take her and look out after her.

For the first time he realized his sister was good for something after all.

4

DRAPE PANTS WERE the thing. Drape pants and wide-brim hats, and long gold key chains, and wide lapel coats, with narrow waists and bulging, padded shoulders, and pointed-toed shoes.

And the chicks wore pompadours, pageboy, and V for Victory hairdos and tight skirts hugging their kneecaps. That's the way it was with their set, the cats dressed up and the chicks sported down. All over the schoolyard you could hear the squeal of Mexican huaraches stomping out rhythm to a boogie-woogie beat.

Freck took off after Beverly and Teacher grinned. "Yeh, that's what we should be doing," he said, "finding us some chicks. Codene and Gene are staked out around here somewhere."

"Aw, you sure they going to show?"

"Yeh, man, I told you she said she was, didn't I? And this fine little stallion Gene's gonna be with her just to meet you."

"Yeh, a lot of good that'll do me," Raymond said. "Having to drag ole little bit around with me everywhere I go."

"I ain't no little bit," Helen said.

"Yeh, Dad, you ought to be glad she came," Jimmy said. "Otherwise you'd still be sitting on your front porch."

"Aw, ain't nobody asked you nothing."

"Aw man, you ain't got to jump salty. I was going to stay here with Helen myself so you and Teacher could go, but I mean if you gonna act like that, well, that's all right too."

"Aw Jack, what you trying to pull?"

"I ain't trying to pull nothing, man. I was just trying to look out for you, but you act like I ain't good enough for your ole sister, or something."

"Naw, it ain't that."

"Well, let's go then," Teacher said. "Man, we ain't got all night."

Raymond looked at Helen. "What do you think, sis?"

"I don't care," Helen said.

Still Raymond hesitated. Then he shook his head. "Just nothing better not go wrong, that's all."

"Aw, man, I told you I'd look out for your sister, didn't I?" Jimmy said. "What more do you want?"

A little later on Sergeant Holt and his partner came through. "So this is what they call a block dance."

"Yeh," Holt said. "As if we didn't have enough to do tonight without them shoving this damn dance off on us, and it ain't even in our district."

"You think they'll really have a gang war out here, Sarge?"

"They always do."

"Well, it looks peaceful so far."

"You just keep your holster open and your eyes peeled," Holt told him. "Come on, I'ma make a cop out of you yet, if it kills me. I still say this is all a waste of time," Holt muttered under his breath. "If you ask me, if the stupid bastards want to kill up each other, why the hell should we care?"

All over the schoolyard Mexican huaraches stomped out rhythm to a boogie-woogie beat.

"You mean to tell me you play quarterback on the football team and can't jitterbug?" Codene told Raymond.

"So he's square," Teacher said laughingly. "He's still my friend, so give him a break."

"Okay, come by my house sometime and I'll learn you how," Codene said.

"Hey," Teacher said. "You don't have to get carried away."

Codene laughed.

Teacher started doing the "Messaround." He pulled Codene up against him until their hips rubbed together.

"Aw shake it, but don't break it," Teacher said.

"Shut up, fool," Codene said, laughing and backing away.

"Aw if I can't make you like it I'll give you your money back," he said.

Codene kept backing away and shaking her shoulders at Teacher. Then everything started shaking.

Raymond stood quietly watching.

"Come on," Teacher said, grabbing Codene by the arm and leading her over to a corner. "I got a bug to put in your ear."

"That Codene ain't nothing but a flirt. She makes me sick," Gene told Raymond. "She's going to get in trouble one of these days. Every night she's got some old mannish thing over to her house."

"Yeh," Raymond said.

"Hey, they're playing something slow now," Codene said, coming back. "You can slow-dance can't you, Raymond?"

Raymond nodded and Codene pulled him out into the crowd of dancers.

"Hey, Codene, you gone do what I asked you?" Teacher yelled at her.

"Maybe," Codene said grinning.

"How 'bout that?" Teacher told Gene. "I introduce him to you and he spends all his time flirting with my date."

"Yeh," Gene said. "Well, I'm going home."

"Hey, what you wanna do that for?"

"If ole greedy Codene wants both of you she can have you," Gene said.

"Hey," Raymond said, seeing Gene and Teacher hurrying across the schoolyard, "where they going?"

"Search me!" Codene said. "Come on, we'd better find out."

Not long after that a new sound crowded out "Hamp's Boogie Woogie."

Ee-oo-weeth! The Hawks announced their invasion of Casa Loma territory.

Dark, doubled-up fists, covered with white handkerchiefs, flashed in the night. Pointed-toed shoes trampled a green-sweatered figure who didn't get away, while wide-eyed girls screamed their approval. Green pullover sweaters, with the yellow C, melted into the crowd and faded away.

The crack of a pistol shot ripped the air and switchblades gleamed under colored lights.

Aw yeh, baby, ee-oo-weeth.

Finally Holt and his partner got through the fleeing crowd over to where the wounded gang member was.

That's when the Hawks earned the reputation of the baddest gang in town.

Holt left his partner with the gang victim and ran into the Hawks on his way over to the callbox to call in what had happened.

Lobo still had the smoking .22 in his hand.

Recognition danced in both their eyes and for a second or two they just stood looking at each other. Then Holt went for his pistol and Lobo squeezed the trigger on his.

An orange streak blossomed in the night air.

Holt clutched at his chest.

Lobo's lips bared back over strong white teeth.

Amazement sagged in Holt's fleshy cheeks.

Lobo's eyes burned red as fire.

. . . you piss blue ink . . .

The orange blossom bloomed again.

Holt pitched forward into the schoolyard. His mouth began to taste blood. Long seconds blurred by, trapped on the impossible thought of a mere boy, a black boy, getting next to him in a jig neighborhood.

Lobo read what the sergeant was thinking.

"Man, come on," Jerome was saying.

Lobo waved them off and they cut out leaving him standing there over the sergeant.

Hate leaped at Lobo from the sergeant's blue eyes.

. . . you piss blue ink . . .

Once more the night flower bloomed.

. . . ee-oo-weeth, you mother. Ee-oo-weeth . . .

All over town the news leaked over the grapevine. The Hawks burned a cop.

5

"MAN, THEM CASA LOMAS is chicken as hell. You should of seen them beating it out of there."

"They wasted one of 'em, huh?" Teacher said.

"Yeh, man," Freck said, propping up against the lamppost. "Man, they walked that cat like he was a pair of shoes."

"You sure he was a Loma, man?"

"Yeh, Jimmy. I'm telling you, man, they worked that cat over something fierce. Stabbed him too."

"How you know so much about what happened when nobody else don't?" Teacher wanted to know.

"Yeh, I suppose you were standing there looking over their shoulders while they were doing it?" Jimmy said.

"Brady told me about it," Freck said.

"So what happened after that?" Raymond wanted to know.

"After that they wasted a cop."

"Yeh," Jimmy said. "I supposed they walked him too?"

"Didn't they!" Freck said. "Like he was a floor mat."

"Aw get up off it, Freck," Teacher said.

"Yeh, Jack. This big ole fat cop comes running over there talking 'bout hey y'all boys, what y'all think y'all doing, and wham, bam, blippity, bop, boom!"

"Yeh," Teacher said. "I suppose Brady told you all that too?"

"I swear to God," Freck said. They stopped listening to him.

"Say, Jim, thanks for looking out for my sister," Raymond told Jimmy. "If you hadn't waited down here on the corner with her until I could take her home, ain't no telling what might of happened."

"Aw, that's all right," Jimmy said. "I told you you didn't have nothing to worry about long as she was with me. If any of them ole jive-time Lomas had messed with her I'd of kicked their ass myself."

"Yeh, them cats ain't nothing but a bunch of mouth," Teacher said. "They couldn't fight they way out a paper bag."

It wasn't long after that a bunch of the Casa Lomas came around the corner. A slim one wearing a zoot suit said, "Hey, Freck, com'ere."

"Yeh, Brady?"

"Which one of these cat's Teacher?"

"Huh?"

"Huh, hell, huss," the dark one wearing a conk said. "Get up off that huh and answer the kiddy's question?"

"Well, I mean—"

"Aw that's all right, papa cool breeze." The dark guy pushed Freck away. Freck kept right on going. "Hey you," he said, walking over to Teacher, sitting down on the curb.

"Who me?"

"Yeh, Ugmo, they call you Teacher, don't they?"

"Well, I mean—"

The dark guy grabbed Teacher by the collar.

"Hey, wait a minute, cuzz, what's going on?" Raymond said.

"You just be cool, dad," Brady said. "Unless you want in too."

There wasn't but six, just two more than them. Raymond looked at Jimmy to give him the eye, but Jimmy started staring at the gutter. Raymond looked around for Freck. Freck was gone.

"The boys tell me your cuzz used one of my boys for a blackboard to write a message on," the dark guy told Teacher.

Sweat started popping out on Teacher's tan face.

"Well, you can be the messenger for the answer," the dark guy said smiling at him.

"But, but, look I don't hardly ever see him," Teacher said. "In fact I don't never see him at all."

The Casa Lomas closed in.

"Hey, Teacher didn't have nothing to do with what came off tonight. He wasn't even there," Raymond said jumping up.

"Man, who the fugg said anything to you?" Brady said.

"Nobody, I was just—"

"Yeh, little nigger, keep your mouth shut," the dark one said, " 'fore the same thing happens to you."

Sweat started running down Teacher's face like water. All he knew was these cats were getting ready to waste him for something he didn't have nothing to do with. "Look, I don't even know my cousin that good, honest," Teacher said. "Look, give him the message," he said pointing at Raymond. "He's a Hawk, he just moved out this way from downtown."

"Hawk, who's a goddamn Hawk?"

Teacher pointed again. They let him go to get at Raymond. Jimmy got his chance to sneak away. Teacher didn't waste any time either.

"Kill that dirty mother," the dark one said. "Don't let that dirty mother get away!"

They didn't.

Walking with my baby, she's got great big feet! long, lean, and lanky like she ain't had nothing to eat . . .

"TROUBLE, TROUBLE, TROUBLE," Mae said. "Raymond, boy, honestly, sometimes you act just like you're plain crazy."

Raymond ran his fingers over the patch on his left eye. "Mama, it wasn't my fault those guys jumped me," he said. "Just 'cause I used to run around with Lobo."

"And how many times have I told you to stay away from Lobo?"

"But I wasn't with him, Mama, honest."

"If I told you once I told you a hundred times, but you wouldn't listen to me, oh no, you think your mother doesn't have a bit of sense."

"Aw, gee whiz."

"You get yourself almost killed and I call the police and what do you do? Sit there like a big, overgrown dummy when they try to find out who did it."

"Aw, Mama."

"Aw Mama my foot. The doctor says you'll be just plain lucky you don't lose the sight of that eye. What in the world's the matter with you?"

Love you, love you just the same . . .

"Well, you know what'll happen if I squeal on 'em. They'd keep after me till they got me again."

"Oh no they wouldn't. They'd lock the ones up who did it and the rest would start acting like they had some sense."

"Yes, they would, Mama. They'd keep after me til they got me."

"Boy, don't tell me, I said they wouldn't, now."

"Okay."

What makes your big head so hard, Mop . . .

"You're just a little half-grown kid, you don't know everything."

"Okay."

"Oh shut up, you make me sick. Why can't you do right like other boys?"

"Well, shoot, Mama, you don't never want nobody to do nothing but sit on the porch all the time. Can't nobody ever do nothing around here, not even Dad."

"Now just what in the world do you mean by that?"

"Well, shucks, I don't never get a chance to practice on my trumpet."

"Boy, you stand there and tell another lie like that and I'll kill you. You do so."

"And Dad said you didn't even want to let him play pro football when he had a chan—"

WHAM! Just like the fat sergeant's hand, his mother's fingers left their impression against the side of his head. WHAM! Twice, almost before she knew it.

"You shut up. I've stood about all of your sass I'm going to take."

Too stubborn to let the tears fall.

Love you, love you just the same . . .

Two white policemen came to their door to take Raymond away.

They said it was in connection with the gang killing of a police officer over at the block dance.

"But my boy wouldn't do a thing like that," Mae said.

Every time a white face showed up in the neighborhood it meant trouble, rent man, bill collectors, police, trouble.

"A young punk like you oughta get his teeth knocked down his throat, worrying his mother like that," one of the policemen said.

"Yeh, what business it of yours?"

"Why you little farthead, just wait'll I get you to the station."

He went into his corner-boy walk, the loose-shouldered, stiff-legged slouch that meant he didn't give a damn. "Anyway, my ole lady don't care nothing 'bout me, she's just putting on an act," he said.

They didn't have any comeback for that. Too stubborn to let the tears fall.

He didn't mean that? He couldn't mean that, Mae thought, watching them get into the squad car and drive away.

Crazy 'bout that woman 'cause Caldonia is her name . . .

"Helen?"

"Ma'am?"

"What are you doing up there?"

"Nothing."

"Well, turn that radio off."

Love you, love you just the same . . . Louis Jordan swore.

"You hear what I said?"

"Yes ma'am."

Caldonia, Caldonia . . . Louis Jordan insisted.

"Then turn that thing off!"

"Mama, that ain't me playing no radio. That's coming from next door."

7

THEY SHOVED HIM into a room with a wild-looking, pudgy-faced guy. It was Teacher.

They made him sit down.

They flexed a rubber hose at him and showed him a .22 revolver. Teacher was in a world of trouble. They said it belonged to his father.

"We found it in a sewer over by the playground. A kid might think he was pretty smart getting rid of it like that, wouldn't he?" a cop under a snapbrim hat said.

Raymond said he didn't know.

The white-haired one wanted to know if he and Teacher weren't tight.

"I just know him, that's all."

Teacher tried getting Raymond's eye, but Raymond turned his head.

"You know what we're holding him for?"

Codene's fingertips on your neck made your flesh crawl.

"Murder."

Codene's body felt warm against you when you danced. She said she was crazy about football players.

"You get the gas chamber in this state for that, you know."

Codene whispered into your ear while you danced. If you ever came by her house it would be to do more than just learn how to jitterbug. Codene laughed and whispered in your ear. Your heart played leapfrog over the moon.

"Pay attention you little butt hole." They jerked him around in the chair. They asked him again whether or not Teacher had been with him at the time the sergeant got wasted. This time, they told him, he had better come up with an answer.

"I just moved out this way from downtown," he told them.

The fat cop pulled him to the edge of the chair by his shirt front. "What kind of answer is that?"

"Guys from downtown and guys from out west ain't never been together in nothing," he told them.

The fat cop relaxed his hold on the front of Raymond's shirt and shoved him back into the chair. "Agh," he said.

Teacher got slapped around for calling Raymond a goddamn liar.

All the way home Raymond heard the fat cop's hand going upside Teacher's head. Teacher could talk his way out of everything so good, let him talk his way out of that.

"I was with him that night, I was," Teacher insisted.

They smiled at him like he was crazy.

"I swear to God, sir. Ask Codene and Gene, they know."

The fat cop yawned. "Yeh, well maybe his father did it."

"No sir!"

"Then you're covering for somebody, boy. Now who is it?" the white-haired one wanted to know.

"Nobody sir, nobody."

The cop under the snapbrim hat stood up. He nodded at the white-haired one and they headed toward the door.

The fat cop shoved his sleeves up over his elbows and swung the rubber hose back and forth in his hands.

Teacher screamed.

The door clicked shut.

"Please sir!"

A thin smile cracked the cop's ruddy face.

"Sir!"

The hose swung in a long graceful arch.

"Sir!"

8

Jimmy and Freck tried the best they could to tell Raymond how sorry they were, only how could you explain something like that?

"It's just that I ain't never been in on nothing like that before," Jimmy said.

"Naw, me neither," Freck said.

Raymond didn't say anything.

"We started to drop by your pad last week," Freck said.

"Yeh, but—hey I guess you heard the cops cut Teacher loose?"

"Aw yeh?" Raymond said.

"Yeh, he told 'em Lobo traded guns with his old man about three years ago."

"Lobo?"

"Yeh," Jimmy said. "You know Lobo's Teacher's cousin."

"Yeh, so I heard."

"Teacher put the finger on him," Freck said, "and the cops picked him up."

"Yeh," Jimmy said, "and Teacher joined the Army to keep the Hawks from getting him."

"Yeh, that Lobo must be out of his mind," Freck said.

"Yeh, that's something, ain't it, burning a cop like that?"

"Yeh," Raymond said, "yeh." He didn't want to talk about it. They took the hint and left.

He didn't get a chance to be alone. You never got the chance to be alone around here. Helen came out of the house and sat down beside him on the porch.

"They're in there talking about you, Raymond," she said.

"So what?"

"They made me come outside so I couldn't hear."

Lobo burned a cop.

"Raymond, was Jimmy really there when those guys jumped on you?"

"Yeh, he was there."

"Wouldn't he help, not even a little bit?"

"Naw."

"I wish he had," Helen said. "I kind of liked him a little bit. Raymond?"

"What? What you got to keep bothering me for?"

Helen's face twisted up and she burst into tears.

"Oh gee whiz, don't you start that," he said.

"Well, why don't you want to talk to me then?"

"Aw look, Helen, there ain't nothing to talk about. Now lay off that bawling, will ya?"

"I know what you're doing. You're thinking 'bout going down there and getting the Hawks to help you clean those Casa Lomas."

"Naw, I ain't, honest."

"Well, what then?"

"Oh, I dunno." He shrugged. "I think I just might try taking off on my own for a while."

"You mean run away from home?"

They were going to send Lobo to the gas chamber and wasn't nothing he could do about it.

"You can't do that Raymond, I won't let you."

"Aw what you care? Don't nobody else round here care what I do."

"Yes they do, Raymond."

"Yeh."

"Grandpa Argustus cares, and Daddy, he cares too."

Lobo didn't play getting called out of his name.

"Even Mama—"

"Naw, she don't care. She don't care nothing about me."

"Yes, she does, Raymond. You know she does."

"Hey, stop that bawling. You ain't nothing but an old crybaby."

"I don't care!"

"Yeh, boy, I might even join the Army."

"You can't, you're only sixteen."

"Yeh, that's all you know. Teacher did, and he ain't no older than me."

Helen jumped up and ran into the house. "Mama, Raymond's running away from home!"

"You ole tattletale!"

They made him come into the house. They gave him a fit. He would never forgive his sister for that, never.

Negro Thug Kills White Cop!
Negro Hoodlum Slays Policeman!

THE DAILY PAPERS gave it front page headlines.

The weekly newspapers couldn't resist it either.

"*St. Loui-iieese Ar-re-go-ooo-ous!*"

"*St. Loui-iieese Call!*"

"Read all about it. Young Carl Logan booked on murder rap!"

And the scandal sheets had their say.

Tennage Gunman Mows Down the Law!

The non-white neighborhoods were invaded by policemen riding streetcars. That didn't prevent a small-scale race riot from igniting in Sherman Park.

All the big-time teenage gang leaders got drafted. "You guys think you so tough, go over there and fight the Japs." New guys stepped in to take their places, new gangs came in: the Deacons, the Sugar Hills, the Turks. The new gangs preached the same old sermon of warfare. The Citizens' Committee for Better Neighborhoods pressured City Hall into hiring more non-white policemen. The sociologists felt it might help alleviate the situation. It didn't.

The guys on the corners kept doing each other in and sometimes when the cops tried going upside their heads they were the ones who ended up getting slapped around. Some of the police, like the ones who patrolled the beat around the Tandy Community Neighborhood, always managed to be going in the opposite direction whenever trouble occurred. He couldn't see that much difference between Sumner and Vashon. Both of them were big schools with lots of noisy students and during his first week out there the Turks jumped off a truck and started shooting at the Sugar Hills who were standing on the southwest corner of Pendleton and Cottage flirting at the chicks walking by. The Turks ran the Sugar Hills down the alley behind Sumner and through the tennis courts of Tandy Community Center, across from Stowe Teachers College, and all the kids coming out of school started yelling and hollering, and pushing and shoving, trying to see what was going on.

Some of the guys stood out in the hall and collected protection money from kids scared of them. Everybody was leery of him over at Sumner because they knew his friend Lobo had burned a cop. Codene wasn't scared of him though. Codene gave him a fit. Every morning she fronted him off before their homeroom class. That didn't hurt her standings any. One day a Casa Loma got stabbed in the lunchroom. The assistant principal called Raymond in and balled him out like he had fingered the cat for the action. The whole school was saying he had. Good night, he got blamed for everything that happened around that joint. In fact the only reason they didn't transfer him to Washington Tech was because the football coach wouldn't stand for it.

He took Helen to the show on Sundays, either the Amytis on Pendleton and St. Ferdinand, or the Circle on Taylor and Easton. The Sugar Hills had the Amytis locked down tight, and if you were a kid you couldn't get in to see the flick without getting a corn stomped on your butt unless you paid protection money. The Sugar Hills never said anything to him though. The Casa Lomas didn't either, when they saw him going into the Circle. These days he had a rep.

The word came out on the corners to be on the lookout for Stiff, because they had made a plainclothes sergeant out of him. Stiff's real name was Lee Clarence Middlepond. They called him Stiff because he had trouble turning his head around, on account of the stab wound he got in the neck when he was blowing the top of the president of the Compton Hills' head off back there in '41. Stiff was a real dark, mean hombre who'd just as soon put his shoe in your tail as look at you, but some of the guys on the corner wouldn't move for Stiff's mama, so you knew they didn't care nothing about him. Guys like that got themselves drafted.

"You guys think you so bad, go over there and fight the Japs." Every time the cops found zoot suits on the corners they got out and started swinging. All over town the cops were swinging. That didn't stop any gang wars.

CARL LOGAN STANDS TRIAL TODAY . . .

Two cars, loaded with white kids, careened over the tracks of the Wellston streetcar line and spat gunfire at the crowd holding down Taylor and Easton Avenues. The guys bragged about how close the bullets had come to missing their heads. Down on Jefferson and Market a stumblebum white man wandered too far from Union Station and got his face slashed.

The early fall temperature shot up over the 100 degree mark for twelve straight days.

CARL LOGAN MUST DIE!

The daily papers screamed it.

OFFICER'S BRUTAL SLAYING ENRAGES CITY!

Day after day the cry went out.

NEGRO CRIME WAVE MUST BE CHECKED!

The editorial pages spilled over with views.

The scandal sheets thought it was a good thing too.

KILLERS'S MOTHER ALL CHOKED UP AT GASSY END PRESCRIBED FOR SON!

The city sweated it out.

"*St. Loui-iieese Ar-re-go-oo-ous! St. Louis Call!* Read all about it! Death sentence given to Negro minor!" brown-skinned news peddlers yelled.

And there was even more exciting news. The Douglases got a letter from one of Wilbur's buddies. It said Wilbur had been badly wounded in action and they weren't sure whether he was going to make it through or not.

10

A GOLDEN-BROWN FOOTBALL arched lazily in the autumn air.

"I go!"

He circled beneath the descending ball, spiraling through the fog of lights milking up the night out at Public School Stadium.

"Hey, hey! Ho, ho! Come on Sumner and let's go!"

Shrill-voiced cheerleaders, in short, tight skirts, screamed their approval. The stands echoed after them.

He cut toward the sideline, swerving past a speedy end who tried to drop him on the ten-yard line.

"Yeh, come on Sumner!"

"Go Number 15!"

He got up to the twenty and Big Joe sprung him loose with a cross-body block that opened up the center of the field, but he had to reverse at the thirty and they chased him all the way back to the fifteen-yard line before he was able to turn the corner and stiff-arm himself out of trouble.

The stands rose to their feet.

"Yea! Go man go!"

Shrill-voiced girls screamed their approval.

When he got to the fifty they knew he was going all the way. Pandemonium broke out on Sumner's side of the stadium. Over on the Kansas City side they sat in stunned silence.

"Who's Number 15?"

"He's that new cat from Vashon."

"Man, sho is a good thing he's playing for us this year."

"Yeh, sho is."

Big Joe booted the ball through the uprights.

"Aw do it to 'em Sumner! Hey, hey! Aw do it to 'em Sumner . . ." Maroon-sweatered cheerleaders spread-eagled the air.

Sumner had a lot to cheer about that season only losing to Lincoln, in East St. Louis where the referee wouldn't let them lose, and Vashon out at Public School Stadium. Everybody at Sumner knew Raymond's name. He, Big Joe, and Chicken made All State that year. A lot of good that did him. Mama never let him out of sight, when he wasn't in school, that whole semester. He didn't even get to walk a chick home in his warmup coat like the other guys did. Codene would have let him walk her home too, after every one of those games, gee whiz!

Codene was really something. She knew it too. "See something you like," she told him. "Get a job and support it."

She laughed at him. She was always laughing at him. "Raymond boy, when your mama going to let you come by my house?"

"Aw, if I came by your house I'd sure do more than learn how to jitterbug."

"Aw, I bet you wouldn't even know what to do."

"Aw yeh, you wanna bet?"

Her eyes mocked him. He was crazy about her. She knew that too. Not in love, just crazy about her in a wild kind of way. No cat in his right mind got any serious thoughts in his head about Codene.

After he blew a solo in the band concert, before the whole student body, in the school auditorium, he really had it made. He'd show 'em. He'd show 'em all, his mama too, one of these days. He'd be just as famous as Grandpa Argustus and Uncle Wilbur; more famous even. His name would be known all over the world. Then Mama would be sorry she treated him the way she did.

One day, when he came home from school, there was an Army sergeant sitting in their living room. The right sleeve of his Eisenhower jacket was pinned to the top of his shoulder and there were campaign ribbons and medals all over his chest. That man was his Uncle Wilbur. It was his right arm that was missing too, his playing arm.

"Well, ain't you going to say you're glad to see me?"

"H-h-hi, Uncle Wilbur."

"Hi, yourself. Hey, what the hell you staring at?"

Wilbur glared angrily at his nephew. "Oh Jesus Christ," he said. He grabbed his overseas cap and overcoat and went out the door.

GOVERNOR SAYS NO REPRIEVE FOR Logan

"Aw come on Jack, lay off that goddamn trumpet, will ya?"

"Wilbur?"

"Well, goddamn, Mae, every time you turn around he's got that horn stuck up to his head. Seems like somebody ought to be able

123

to get a little peace and quiet around here every now and then anyway."

"Raymond!" Mae opened the door in the hallway over the steps leading into the basement. "Raymond!"

"Mama?"

"You stop that fooling around and come on upstairs. You're disturbing your Uncle Wilbur and me too."

"Aw."

"You don't need to practice at home anyway, you get enough practice at school, and I'm sure you can find more valuable things to do with your time than fool around with that silly ole horn."

"Aw Mama!"

"Aw Mama my foot. You come on up here. I want you to go to the store for me anyway."

"Well, gee whiz!"

"Come on, boy, I got a job for you," Argustus told him one day when he got home from school.

"A job? Doing what?" Raymond wanted to know.

"Never you mind. It's good hours, three-thirty to five-thirty every day after school. You'll like it. Hurry up, you don't wanna be too late your first day."

"But—"

"Raymond, boy, you just march yourself over to that job your grandfather got for you. With you working your daddy won't have to give you an allowance, and Lord knows money don't grow on trees."

"Aw Mama."

"Don't you Aw Mama me. That's the first sensible thing Argustus's done since coming to stay with us, so you just take your little ole self on over there and see about that job."

Well, gee whiz!

They took the Easton bus and got off on Sarah Street. Then they took the Sarah bus to Maffit and walked over to the two-family residence in the middle of the block. A short, dark-eyed lady, with gray hair, came down the steps from the second floor and opened the door.

"Well, my Lord, he doesn't look anything like the little devil you made him out to be, Argustus," the lady said.

"Raymond, this is Ida Perkins. The sweetest little gal this side of heaven," Argustus said, kissing her on the cheek.

"Just call me Ida," she said. "Come on upstairs, you two. Raymond, I bet you're just starved for some ice cream and cake. Young folks always are."

"Well, boy, how do you like your new job?" Argustus said after Raymond had started digging into the piled up saucer of vanilla ice cream and chocolate cake Ida had insisted he take.

"Well, Grandpa, I mean gee whiz, I don't even know what it is."

"Well, I'll be goddamn," Argustus said. "I guess you don't at that." He slapped his knee and broke out laughing.

"Argustus, shame on you," Ida said.

"Aw yeh, well look, boy, this is how it is. This job pays fifty cents an hour, see. You can't get no more than that 'cause you ain't worth it." Argustus broke out laughing again. "Yeh, and you got to put in your two hours, every day after school, or else'n you don't get paid. And you know what you got to do?"

Raymond shook his head.

"Bring your horn over here and practice, that's what," Argustus said. "That shouldn't be hard to do, should it? I mean, hell, Mae won't let you practice over on Cora, noway."

"Yes sir, I mean no sir, I mean for real, Grandpa?"

" 'Course he does," Ida said.

"Gee, thanks, Grandpa."

"Don't thank me, thank Ida. This was all her idea."

"Well goodness sakes," Ida said. "We can't have a future musician neglecting his practicing, can we? I mean what would this world be coming to if we allowing a thing like that to happen?"

"Gee thanks, Miss Ida, thanks," he said. Suddenly he wanted to get out of here, because even though it was the end of December, it seemed springtime was just around the corner and he felt guilty feeling so happy on the day his best friend was going to the gas chamber.

"Sunday morning *Post 'Nnnnn Glooo-ooooobe!*"

Argustus bought the Sunday papers late that Saturday night. The headlines of the papers rocked the sockets of their eyeballs.

... Colored Cop Killer Wins Last Minute Reprieve!
... Governor Pardons Negro Cop Killer!

"RAYMOND DOUGLAS, for goodness sakes. What you doing walking over this way?"

"Hi, Gene. I'm going over to my aunt's."

"You got a aunt who lives over here?"

"Well she's just my play aunt, but I go over there every day after school."

"Oh? Where is that?" Gene wanted to know.

"On Sarah, right off Maffit, in the middle of the block."

"I live right around the corner from there," Gene said.

"Aw yeh?"

"Uh-huh. Why didn't you tell me you played football?"

Raymond shrugged.

"Quarterback too." She grinned at him.

She had big, slightly bowed legs, and all the other stuff the fellas were crazy about.

She gave him the once-over out the corner of her gray cat eyes.

Gene lived in a small frame house that sat back in the middle of a yard surrounded by a green picket fence. "Wanna stop in a second and see what the ole place looks like?"

"Well, I have to be where I'm going by three-thirty."

"You still got about ten minutes."

It was a sin if you wasn't married.

His hands did things they had never done to a girl before.

The Bible said you shouldn't.

Argustus and Aunt Ida would be mad at him and maybe wouldn't let him come over and practice any more.

"I really got to be on my way."

She just looked at him. The hell with what the Bible said.

When he finally got to Aunt Ida's there was a note on the door. The note said that Argustus and Aunt Ida had gone shopping and the key was downstairs. Every Thursday Aunt Ida and Argustus went shopping. Every Thursday he spent with Gene down on her living-room rug. He knew it was wrong, but he didn't care, and after a while he stopped worrying about what the good Lord was going to do about it. He saved up fifteen dollars and bought a maroon slipover sweater to sew his varsity football letter on. Gene wore his football sweater all the time. A lot of guys tried to steal his ole lady from him. They thought she was real tough, just because she was light, bright, damn near white, and had long, brown, straight hair. He didn't see no big deal in that; in fact he thought she was kind of plain looking, but she sure was stacked. Yeh, man, real stacked where it counted the most.

And ole Codene was always meddling him. Bumping into him in the hallway when there was plenty of room to get by, and pulling her skirt down over her knees whenever he looked across the aisle at her in their homeroom. Codene was the kind of dame a guy would like to spend the rest of his life around, but couldn't trust long enough to marry.

13

THEN TRACK SEASON CAME and he lost his girl to Alphonso Jones, who was the captain of the track team and held the state record in the high and low hurdles. He never appreciated Gene until she was gone. He had never had to take her anywhere, or buy her anything, and every Thursday he got to go inside her house. He got so he'd stare at Gene in their English class, whenever he thought she wasn't looking. He'd stare and remember those times down on the living-room rug.

Codene teased him more than ever after Alphonso stole his girl away.

In May they had a school dance, at three o'clock on the second-floor hallway, and as usual Codene found some kind of way to front him off in front of everybody. She gave him lessons on how to jitterbug, and talked about him like a dog, but he forgave her on the first slow record. Codene danced so close to him he could hear her breathing. He could feel it too, the front of her sweater moving up and down his chest.

Codene was interested in modeling clothes and going for rides in long, slinky cars, and entertaining folks in the patio (in the California home her parents were buying after she finished high school), and swimming and lounging on the beach; stuff like that. Codene could dance her can off too. All the guys gathered around to get a chance to jitterbug with her. They liked to slow-dance with her too. She sure was a big tease. She handed all the guys a story. Yeh, that Codene had a line for everybody. What chance did a guy like him have with a dame like that?

"Naw, no thanks, Johnny," he heard her tell her dancing partner. "Raymond's walking me home."

Johnny had a car. That's all he could think of. Johnny had a car.

"What you looking at me like that for?" Codene asked him after the dance was over and she joined him on the sidelines.

"Huh? Nothing."

"You are going to walk me home, aren't you?"

"Yeh, sure."

"Are you sure you can? Maybe your mama won't let you, like during football season."

"Aw, what you talking about. I used to walk Gene home, didn't I?"

"Yeh, you sure did, didn't you?"

Anyway that's the way it started between him and Codene.

He didn't have time to walk her home after school every day and get to practice on time, but it didn't really matter, because they weren't really going together anyway. They were just friends and every Sunday he took her to the show. Man, he sure was glad his mama didn't insist on making him take Helen with them.

Codene was good at breaking down movies. She knew a lot about music too, but she wouldn't talk about it with him. She let him do all the talking like his mouth was a prayerbook or something. She made him mad doing that. He would have liked her to have something to say about what he was interested in, every now and then anyway, but all she ever talked about that he was interested in was football, and all she said about that was she was afraid of him getting hurt, and she didn't want him to get hurt, so what kind of conversation was that?

The last month of school went down real crazy. Aunt Ida let him bring a few guys over on Saturday night and they had a ball. He and Willy, and Benny Berry, and Peter Rabbit. They had their own little jam session and Argustus sat in and showed them a lot of tricks. His ole grandpa could really play that trumpet, kind of ole-fashioned, and sometimes a little corny, but man he could whale! Each Saturday they had that jam session over at Aunt Ida's. He wouldn't have missed it for anything in the world.

"Hey, Raymond, you going to the Hi-Y dance Saturday night?" Codene asked him one Monday morning in their homeroom.

"Well, naw, I wasn't planning on it. I usually practice on Saturday with Peter Rabbit and them over my aunt's house."

"Oh."

"Well, Codene, ain't nothing for you to jump salty about."

"Who's jumping salty?"

"Well, you sure the heck sound like it."

"Raymond Douglas, do you mean to stand there and tell me you think I'd get mad at you just because you'd rather practice on your silly ole trumpet than go to the dance with me?"

"Well, good night Codene. If that's what you wanted me to do why didn't you say so?"

"Say what?"

"Take you to the dance."

"Who asked you to take them anywhere?"

"Well, you just said—"

"I'll have you know, Raymond Douglas, that I don't have to ask any boy to take me nowhere, least of all a big ole jive-time square like you."

"Well, I was just—"

"Aw go jump in the lake!"

He told his grandpa about it. His grandpa gave him some advice. He tried it on Codene.

"Go over to your aunt's and listen to you practice while there's a dance going on, you kidding?"

It was plain to see his grandpa might know a whole lot about music, but didn't know a thing about women. Saturday night was lousy. He couldn't concentrate on one tune, all the way through, the whole night long. Chicken Curry had taken Codene to the Hi-Y dance. He wondered what they were getting into.

"How was the session?" Codene asked him next Monday morning.

"Oh—that. Yeh, well, it came off all right."

"When you going to have the next one?"

"Next Saturday."

"You going to come by and pick me up?"

"Huh? Well, yeh, but I didn't think you wanted to come."

"Why not?"

"You know, last week?"

"What's that got to do with this Saturday?"

"Well, nothing, I just thought—"

"Raymond Douglas, you just like to pick fights with me."

"Naw, I don't."

"Well, I don't see why you go around inviting folks to things if you don't want them to come."

"Who don't want nobody to come?"

"Well, what you fussing at me about then?"

"Well, gee whiz Codene, I ain't fussing. All I wanted to know was could you be ready by eight o'clock?"

"When?"

"Saturday night?"

"Yeh, I guess so."

Boy, maybe his grandpa wasn't so dumb after all.

Argustus and Codene hit it off right away. "Boy if I was twenty years younger I'd steal that spring chicken right away from you."

"Aw, we just good friends, Grandpa."

"Sure you are." Argustus winked at Raymond and Codene.

"Argustus, stop that kidding and act your age," Ida told him.

Argustus pulled Ida down on the sofa and kissed her on the cheek. "You know what, baby, if I'd met you ten years ago, we'd probably be married by now," he said.

"Argustus honey, I've got news for you," Ida said.

"Huh?"

"Better late than never," Ida told him.

Argustus started coughing.

Codene sat silently listening to Raymond and his group play. She had been expecting something, she wasn't sure what, but it certainly hadn't been the way Raymond could play that trumpet. She had heard him play before, during the school band concerts and during school assemblies, but it hadn't been anything like this. Raymond was alive on that horn, everything about him was alive. She got the feeling he was more alive even than when he was running with a football, and it frightened her. The others could play, too, and Raymond's grandfather was so much fun he had her in stitches, but nobody dominated that room like Raymond Charles Douglas. She said the name again to herself silently. Raymond Charles Douglas. All night long she said it.

He grabbed her at her gate and kissed her quickly before she could move away.

"Why Raymond, I didn't know you cared."

He held her so close he almost squeezed the life out of her.

"Raymond, boy, you better go home."

Next day he brought a package by her house. "I thought I'd bring this by. I just got it back from the cleaners," he said.

Codene opened the bundle and took out his letter sweater.

"I thought you might want to wear it sometime," he said.

"Humph, after ole Gene used to wear it all the time, and got it all out of shape too, I bet."

"Well, yeh, but that was a long time ago—I mean—"

She smiled at him. "Boy, you sure took your own sweet time bringing it around, didn't you?"

"Huh?"

"Never you mind. See you."

"Yeh, see you, Codene."

"**O**DE-ode-ode-ooo."

"ODE-ODE-ODE-OOOO."

"Ode-ode-ode-ooo."

"ODE-ODE-ODE-OOO."

"It's the Sumner boogie."

". . . THE SUMNER BOOGIE."

"It's a crazy song."

". . . CRAZY SONG."

The drum roll was back, trumpet scream, the hard herd of cool cats cutting a rug with hip chicks in the middle of the stadium aisles. Ticketless kids scaled the stadium walls, or squeezed through the bent iron bars of the stadium gates, the same as they had last year. Stadium attendants chased the kids as they poured in. Getting chased was almost as much fun as seeing the game. There were other kicks to be had too. You could get all kind of kicks at a night public high school football game. Babes, fights, drinks; all kinds of kicks. That was why everybody went.

Blue-sweatered Hawks swaggered through the crowd on Sumner's side of the stadium. "Get out the way, moafugg. I come to see my boy play."

The string of wooden benches bulged with people standing in their seats and down beneath them, on the cinder track surrounding the football field, cheerleaders bounced up and down. The game had started and the ball was spotted on Sumner's own eighteen-yard line. Number 15 faked a handoff and galloped around end, hiding the pigskin against his thigh like a bootleg expert; something his father had taught him how to do. He romped ten yards down the sidelines, and the stands went wild, suddenly realizing what he was up to.

"Go boy, go!"

Then the other team found out.

"Yeow-hoo!"

"Go on fool, run that football!"

He saw the fifty-yard stripe speeding by beneath his feet and someone hit him from behind, sending him tumbling into the air. He pawed at space with his cleats and got his legs under him again, so that when he hit the ground he was able to land on the ball of one foot, stumbled, for three or four steps, catch his balance and take off again.

"Yeow-hoo!"

"Ee-oo-weeth!"

The safety man grabbed his jersey and rode him ten yards before he managed to shake away. That slowed him up long enough for them to catch him on their own fourteen-yard line.

"Look out Raymond!"

Cheers exploded in the stands as Number 15 got up from beneath the mob of players and kicked the kinks out of his legs.

"Codene, girl, open your eyes."

"Is he hurt?"

"Girl, I don't know?"

"Aw, he's all right. Codene, girl, you crazy."

The maroon and white huddle broke up and the players spiraled out in the shape of an S as they lined up for the next play.

"Ho, ho!"

Raymond bent over Harvey James shouting out signals.

"COME ON SUMNER AND LET'S GO."

Raymond faked a handoff to their fullback Andrew Jones and pitched out to Chicken Curry hurrying around right end with Clem Steel pulling guard and their left half Eli Davis out front running interference. A charging end fought through and Chicken Curry bounced off him and caromed down across the six-yard stripe before they piled him up.

"Boy, ole Chicken sure do play some football," Jimmy told Helen who was wearing his sweater in the stands.

"So does number 15," the girl next to Helen said. "Girl, is that really your brother?"

Helen nodded.

"He goes with Codene McCluskey," Jimmy told her, "and she's the leader of the majorettes, so I don't think he would spare time for a little ole freshman like you."

"Oh, how would you know? Anyway, all I said was he was a good football player."

Jimmy looked at the girl's dark eyes flashing in a complexion like coffee that was almost all cream. The little broad had high cheekbones, and curly jet-black hair, and one of those round dimples parting the center of her chin. "Jetan Jeffries, you know what? I bet if you was a little bit older, and a little bit more, you know," he drew some curves with his hands, "you just might be able to steal ole Raymond away from that dame."

"Oh shut up, Jimmy. You make me sick," the girl said.

Raymond sneaked for a touchdown while Lincoln was busy piling up on Chicken. "Fools, can't y'all see I ain't got no football?" Chicken said.

"That boy's a football-playing fool," Argustus told Hosea.

"Yeh, well, he don't do bad."

Mae squeezed Hosea's arm.

After the game was over Helen introduced her friend to Raymond.

"Raymond this is Jehtahn."

"Jeh-tahn? How you spell that?" Raymond wanted to know.

"Jetan," she told him. Codene tugged on his arm. "Come on Raymond, let's go."

Codene and Jetan flashed eyes at each other.

He rode home with Codene on the Cass Street car line.

"Raymond, how you manage to keep going like that after they hit you so hard?"

"I guess I just don't know when I got enough," Raymond said.

Codene kissed him in front of her house and ran inside before he could do anything about it.

15

THEY HAD AN undefeated season. When they beat Washington Tech he got to feel the front of his sweater with Codene inside, and when they whipped Vashon 13-0, that Thanksgiving, Codene invited him over that night for dinner.

Codene's folks even worked on Thanksgiving. She said all they cared about was money. She showed him all through the house, pointing out the expensive furniture they had. It made her mad that her folks would rather work triple time than eat Thanksgiving dinner with her.

"Yeh, well, if they wanna work every holiday, let 'em, see if I care. Hey Raymond, you want some wine?"

"Aw, Jim, I don't know, Codene. I don't think I got no room behind that big dinner."

"My mama can really cook, can't she?"

"Yeh, boy, she sure can."

"My mama didn't cook, I did," Codene said.

"You did?"

"Uh-huh. Mama taught me how when I was still a little-bitty 'thing before the war," Codene said. "I use to have a lot of fun with my folks before the war."

She brought him back a cool glass of Virginia Dare. It tasted a lot better than the white port he used to drink with Lobo and them on the corners.

The wine had his head flying like a balloon. Codene looked like she was feeling pretty good too. They started messing around. He mashed her between him and the couch. "Raymond don't, you'll give me a baby."

"Naw, I won't."

She wanted to tell him she wanted his baby, but you couldn't tell a boy nothing like that. She wanted to tell him he scared her.

Every time he played football, or blew his horn, he scared her. You couldn't tell a boy that neither.

*H*E AND CHICKEN made All State again that year. Frankie Boy and Jerome grabbed almost as much space in the papers as he did. Frankie Boy and Jerome got sent up to Boonville Training School. Mickey took over in the Hawks when that happened.

"Eee-oo-weeeeth, you mothers! Eeeoooowweeeth!"

He got eleven scholarship offers and Chicken got thirteen. Every senior on that team got scholarship offers.

"Raymond?"

"Sir?"

"I think the State University of Iowa is your best deal."

"Yes sir. I guess so."

"The pros'll be sure to notice you at a Big Ten school," Hosea said.

"Yes sir."

"But you make up your own mind about it. It's your decision to make."

"Okay Dad, I will." Shoot, the heck he would. He had gotten that scholarship from Juilliard just like Mr. Austin, the band director, said he would. But, he knew he couldn't take it. For one thing it only offered tuition and board for a year, and even Lincoln, his mother and dad's alma mater, offered more than that. Besides, they didn't play football at Juilliard, and his dad wanted him to play football. Maybe he could major in music at Iowa? His mama wouldn't like it though; naw, his mama wouldn't like it. He guessed he'd just have to settle for Physical Ed, and try to sneak a music course or two in every now and then.

"Too bad you didn't get a scholarship to UCLA," Codene told him.

"Yeh."

"Yeh, we could of had a ball."

Codene never let him close to her again after Thanksgiving, but he didn't complain. You didn't press your luck with a goddess who had come down out of heaven long enough for you to make love to her.

*T*HE FLAMING NOTES of Argustus's trumpet bellowed up to haunt Mae again. The blues train rode the path of Mama's scream in the freight yard. Yesterday's voices punctured back through the veiled screen of memory.

"Hey, save me a piece of that nigger woman!"

"Hey, quit shoving it's my turn now!"

"Aw she likes it! Don't y'all like it? Tell him y'all likes it y'all black bitch!"

Juilliard had sent a one-year scholarship to Raymond. She was dumb-struck with amazement. Did she carry an Anderson curse in her blood so that it was transmitted to her offspring through her genes? She jammed a pencil between her teeth to stop her chin from trembling. She was besieged by another attack of headaches. She had pain in her head the way she hadn't had for fourteen years. Juilliard sending a scholarship to Raymond? He was that good? She started shutting herself off in the bedroom. She started spending all her time down on her knees praying.

18

J ETAN WAS ONLY FIFTEEN, but she was cute and and she liked to be seen in his company, so he didn't exactly hate her. But all the girls were nice to him that first summer he got back from Iowa, so he didn't exactly spend all his time with her either. He didn't like going to Iowa. He felt the way a bug under a microscope must feel after everybody got through picking, and squeezing, and prying to see what made him tick. He wished he had gone on down to Tennessee A & I with Chicken. (Ole Chicken had made first string his first year out.) He wouldn't play for the A squad until next season, and they were talking about switching him to left half rather than quarterback, so what the hell he didn't see no big deal on it, but everybody else did, just because he was playing for the Big Ten. Everybody was pulling for him, everybody was counting on him to make a good example and show those white folks you could do anything they could once you got the chance, so he had to get good grades and make All America, or else everybody back home would be through with him. He would be that hoodlum again, that boy who used to run with that cop killer. Boy, if Buddy Young couldn't make All America, how the hell they expect him to? He'd better do it though. Everybody was counting on him, especially his old man. Well, at least he'd made it through the first part all right. He got all B's and one A so that he made honor roll his first semester and right now everybody was crazy about him. Everybody but Mama, but he didn't pay that too much mind. You couldn't ever expect to please Mama no matter what you did.

19

. . . well the blues is my companion, 'cause it's you I hate to lose . . .

LORD, AMERICA DROPPED the atomic bomb on the Japanese and the war was over. They couldn't be satisfied with one bomb, they had to drop two, as if that would bring back Wilbur's arm, or the dead back to life, or all the broken homes the war had traded money for. And people stayed drunk for weeks. Mae heard how the colored folks big-timed in the bars around town. She heard about how white gals went splashing around naked in the lakes out at Forest Park, and how white men in that town carried on too, but she wasn't surprised about that. She knew all about how white men acted, and white women too. They had shown her how in that 1917 massacre in East St. Louis, Illinois. Now her son was going to school among them, because Hosea insisted upon it, and she had heard from reliable sources that Raymond had been seen around town in a few taverns himself. One of them even told her that at one place he had gotten up on the stand with the band to play. None of her prayers seemed to do any good anymore. She began to start wondering if they ever had? Lord, sweet Jesus, have mercy. Lord, I'm so tired, Lord. My soul case's tired, Lord. My little boy is a good boy, Lord. Please don't let him get filled with all this filth and corruption. Please save him, Lord, save him. And I got a little girl too, Lord, and I'm so weak, Lord, and the strain's so hard, Lord, and long, Lord, so awful long.

Raymond brought his grades home that summer and she aged before their eyes. Her faced lined out and her hair turned gray and she got sick; so sick she couldn't get out of bed, but no doctor could

tell them what was wrong. Raymond brought his grades home that
summer and she stopped speaking to him.

20

HE GIGGED ALL OVER TOWN that summer, and he didn't tell
anybody at home about it, not even Argustus, because he didn't
want his mama to know, and when he couldn't get a gig with some
group, he'd go someplace and sit in. He became a regular fixture
at Club Riviera, the Masonic Hall, Tom Powell Post, Waiters' Club,
Bird Cage Lounge, Show Bar, the Palace Garden, and the Harlem
Club in Brooklyn, Illinois. They let him play. He had a beat out of
this world. He could play the bell off that horn. Only thing, he was
mostly technique and so far out that a lot of it wasn't together yet;
but there was no denying that beat, no denying that rhythm, no
denying that soul, and all the chicks were after him, who were out in
the streets now and remembered him from his high school football-
playing days, and some who wanted to know more of him because
of his horn, and he got a few offers from cats around town to join
up as a regular with their band, and when summer was through he
almost died, knowing he had to go back to the cold, sterile class-
rooms of Iowa University and get the microscope test again so that
everybody back home would be happy including his ole man.

21

. . . I'm gone pack myself a suitcase—move on down the line . . .

RAYMOND BROUGHT HIS GRADES home that next semester
and his mama started screaming and wouldn't stop. And she was
like that in the ambulance all the way over to Homer G. Phillips
Hospital, and three weeks after they brought her there they told
them she shouldn't be in a ward with patients who weren't suffering
from a mental illness, and after that every time they went to visit
her it was in a ward called Two South.

He couldn't go back to school behind that. He didn't care if he
never set foot inside another school. He couldn't help thinking that
his going away to school had helped cause it all. He kept thinking
about the way she had acted toward him last summer when he
showed her the grades he had made. His mama had always been
after him to make good grades, and he had made them, all the way
through grade school and high school, but she didn't seem happy
about his making honor roll at Iowa. In fact she acted like he had
done something wrong, something real bad, which she would never
forgive him for. He didn't understand it. He had elected to major
in Physical Education, hadn't he? And he hadn't taken but one
music course, and he had gotten all B's and even one A, so what
did she have to be mad about? Then when he'd brought his grades
home the last time, she had started screaming at him. She kept
screaming that the devil had his soul. He couldn't understand that.
He hadn't been in any trouble in years now, and she said the devil
had Argustus's soul, and Wilbur's too, but that he wasn't going to
get hers. Poor Mama, it didn't do any good to visit her. She wouldn't
never say nothing to him. She always acted like he wasn't even
there. The only ones she would talk to were Hosea and Helen

and then you couldn't understand what she was talking about, she rambled so. He didn't want to go see her anymore. He supposed he would have to though. Mama, I didn't mean to do what I done. Mama, I'm sorry. Hear, Mama? I'm sorry. The only thing was he didn't know what he was supposed to be sorry for. The only thing he could figure out was that maybe she hadn't liked it because the only A's he had gotten on his report card had been in his three-hour music course, Introduction to the Theory of Harmonic Structure. But why she should get so upset about something like that, he couldn't say.

So he didn't go back to school. He started gigging, around town, any place he could. He even made a couple of sets over in East St. Louis at the Red Top, playing cornbread music for the boogie-woogie crowd, but a cat could only take so much of that kind of stuff without snapping his wig, so he turned most of those kinds of gigs down. Every now and then he played the Blue Flame, and Club Manhattan, and the Faust Club on the East Side, but his steady gig was with Charlie Powers's group at the Showbar out on Delmar and Taylor where the reefer smell was as thick as cigarette smoke and smack flowed all around on the corner. Smack, that was junk you shot yourself with through a needle that laid you up about four stories above heaven. He didn't fool with smack, he had too much sense for that, but he did let ole Johnny Knight talk him into trying a joint on for size. Ole Johnny blew tubs for Charlie and wasn't much older than Raymond. Ole Johnny was a knockout. He had all the waitresses in the place crazy about him, and the chicks who came into the joint dug him too. All the cats thought the chicks were coming in to dig Charlie, 'cause he was such a gas on tenor, but Charlie was on smack and stayed too high most of the time to dig broads and it was Johnny they came looking for, and after Raymond joined, some of them came looking for him.

Reefer was a gas, it took you sailing way out where your mind looked back to find out what your body was doing. Yeh, reefer was a gas, a natural petrol. Man, he started getting high all the time, when he wasn't on the stand. You couldn't perform on the stand worth a damn behind no reefer. At least he couldn't. A lot of cats said it didn't bother their performance none, but he didn't believe them. He left whisky alone. Whisky was a lame high that didn't come nowhere close to tea. You could tell what was to a cat just by looking at the drinks in front of him. If he bought beer that meant he was either kicking some reefer, or broke as hell, and just as square. If he bought whisky the chances were he was just square. If he kept on buying whisky, that made you sure of it. They had a lot of square cats hanging around the Showbar. They had lot of square babes around there too. Man, some of those babes were so square they thought marijuana was dope and you could get a habit behind it. It was tough getting the kind of ole lady you could appreciate around that place; that's why he spent so much time with Jetan. Jetan dug whatever he dug. He didn't let her get high though. He told her she'd have to wait until she got out of high school and grew up before she could do the things he was doing and travel in the circles he was moving in.

"Shoot, you ain't but four years older than me."

"You're still too young."

"Yeh, well I know a lot of other guys that don't think so."

They got to necking a lot, in her front parlor, after her mother had gone to bed. Her mother trusted him. They had a lot of fun, and when Jetan and Helen graduated in '48 they came up to the Playground to hear him play. Jetan was a knockout. She told everybody that he was her ole man and he let her. Jetan had gotten fine as wine and ripe for plucking. He'd never noticed she was that fine, maybe because he'd never seen her all dressed up like that before. She had dressed like a girl in high school even when he took her to the movies, but graduation night she was all slinked down like a woman, a hell-of-a bundle of woman too. She sat for hours just listening to him play, looking at him with her chin in her hands and her elbows propped up on the table. She wouldn't dance with anybody the whole night long.

"Raymond," Helen told him once, during an intermission. "You think Daddy'd have a fit if I went down to Tennessee A & I on a track scholarship?"

"Track scholarship?"

"Uh-huh, didn't you know your sister's the fastest runner Sumner's got?" Jetan said.

"She means fastest girl runner, only Sumner never had a girl track team. Tennessee has though and Miss Collins, our gym teacher, used to go there."

"Oh yeh."

"Uh-huh, she got Helen a scholarship there," Jetan said. "Boy, your sister can really run."

The way his sister had blossomed out, he could imagine her more at home modeling clothes than running track. Everybody else seemed to think so too, the way the cats kept beelining over to their table asking her up for a dance. "Well, naw I don't see why he should mind," Raymond said. "In fact, he oughta kind of go for it. He always did want an athlete in the family. It might as well be you."

"You don't think running track is too unladylike then?"

"Look, sis, believe me, there ain't nothing unladylike about you."

She kissed him.

"Whale on, Jack," the guy at the next table told him. "Jim, I sure wish I played something myself. Man, this stud's got two ole ladies, and here I can't get even one."

That didn't make Jetan and Helen feel bad.

"Give me one more year," Raymond told Jetan. "One more year, and I'll be in the bigtime. You'll see."

Every spare chance he got, he spent over at Jetan's house making love. He never took it too far though. Her mother trusted him and anyway, there wasn't any hurry. He had plenty of girls.

One day he went over to Jetan's house without bothering to call on the phone.

Tack was over there. Tack was taking a pre-med course at Howard University these days. He talked with an eastern accent, and had started wearing a crew cut instead of bangs all plastered down over his head with Murray's pomade. Jetan couldn't get over them knowing each other. It seemed Tack was an old boyfriend who had dropped in to visit her during the Easter holidays. Jetan started crying and told Raymond she couldn't see him anymore. That didn't make no kind of sense, but he left because he was mad.

He didn't see Jetan for three months, when he went over to her house after hearing, from the grapevine, she had swallowed a watermelon. He went over to her house and it was true. Jetan was pregnant as hell. He couldn't get over it.

"What are you going to do."

Tack says he'll marry me soon as he graduates."

"But that'll be years from now."

"So, it'll be years from now."

"I'd been sort of planning on asking you to marry me myself."

"Oh, Raymond, don't say that."

"But I had, I told you it would only take me about another year to hit it big."

His standing there making her cry wasn't helping solve anything. He cut out. The sidewalk was the sound of kids playing hide-spy.

"There's a bird on the fence, must I kill it?"

"Naw."

The hell with broads anyway; they were beyond comprehension. First there was Codene who hadn't; then there was Jetan, who had. Codene a virgin and Jetan a tramp. Who the hell would of ever thought that? But, naw, he shouldn't say that. Jetan was a long way from a tramp. You couldn't call a broad a tramp just because she had the misfortune to get knocked up by a jive-time stud like Tack. He supposed a lot of it was his fault. He didn't know why, but he supposed it was.

"There's a bird on the fence, must I kill it?"

"Naw."

Light fell down before darkness just as though nothing had happened.

"I ain't gone count but one more time."

Stars came out same as always and the jive-time moon bobbled along like a eggwhite sailboat in a purplish sky.

"There's a bird on the fence, must I kill it?"

"Naw!"

"Ready or not here I come!"

His whole style on horn changed. He stopped trying to execute tricky phrases and cute clichés. He bombarded his emotions inward, into himself, and breathed out feelings on his horn like a sanctified soul shouting for salvation in a Baptist church and the blue note became his calling card. Fast, slow, hot, cold, it didn't matter to him what the tempo was, the frequency was all the same, blue. Blues for Lobo, and Codene, and Jetan, and Wilbur, and his mother, and all the crumb-snatchers along Papin Avenue who looked at the movie houses with bulging eyes, and the gangs on the corners, and the two-dollar prostitutes on the levee bars, and Biddle Street and Franklin Avenue, and the crowded tenement flats that stretched all the way from downtown clear out to the foothills of Cora Avenue, and his tone mellowed out huge as the soul of a bottomless well-spring pouring hot lava down an indifferent mountainside, and the word got around.

"Man, you hear 'bout that stud on trumpet out at the Showbar?"

"Naw Jack, what's to him?"

"I can't tell you, man, you got to hear him for yourself."

"Aw yeh, man?"

"Yeh man."

And the guys came down to see, some stagging, some dragging their chicks along.

"Man, that stud plays like hog guts and pea juice."

"Like the color of blues, man."

"Yeh, man, like the color of blues making it from a train whistle."

And the big band of Bennie Williams blew into town one night, for a gig at the Riviera, and caught him on a set. Bennie and his boys had dropped in to hear Charlie play. Charlie had been with them until he kept staying so loaded they couldn't depend on him anymore. They had come to hear Charlie. They hadn't known a thing about that new boy on trumpet.

That new boy on trumpet showed them a few things. That new boy on trumpet cried on the stand and the tears rolled out in big, bubbly notes weaving a spell so powerful you could almost stick out your hand and feel the weight of the blues.

"Hey, Jack, where this cat come from?"

"You got me," Bennie said. "Go on, boy, play it. Yeh, ride it. Ride the drawls off that thing."

And when the Bennie Williams aggregation left town they took Raymond with them.

See, Jetan, I told you. Just a year. Just one little year. But you weren't even listening.

. . . yeh, pack my suitcase—move on down the line . . .

HE PLAYED WITH BENNIE for two years, right up to the time he got drafted for that goof they called police action in Korea, and he should have had a ball, traveling all over the country from coast to coast, playing for packed houses everywhere they went. He didn't though. He saw the cities, like a man in a trance, like a stud getting high and going to the movie to dig a flick. He stayed moody, he stayed blue, and that didn't make Bennie and his boys sorry, 'cause his horn was saying what they wanted it to say. Only he seemed to be aware that he couldn't go on like that forever. He met all kinds of broads. He shacked up with all kinds of broads too, blondes, brunettes, redheads. He got to the point where white broads didn't excite him anymore, and he had Japanese babes too, and Chinese, and Mexican, but mainly he had a great big ball of loneliness all to himself.

And the service, that was a drag too, mainly because they

wouldn't let him go overseas and he had to spend all of his time down on a jive-time base in Virginia, where a lot of paddy studs still didn't know that boots were human. Back under the microscope again, yeh, and the only reason they let him in special service was because he stood six-foot-one, weighed one hundred and ninety-five pounds. He made All Army quarterback too. His old man was proud of that. He hadn't given his old man much to be proud of, yeh, but what the hell, each man had to live his own life.

He got out of service late in the summer of '52 and it started all over again. They came through St. Louis early in January for three big nights, Thursday, Friday, and Saturday at Club Riviera. Things had changed back home. For one thing the Showbar had changed its name to the Playground and gone out of business, his ole pal Johnny Knight had gotten killed in a car accident, and Charlie had gotten busted on a narcotics rap. Not only that, but some damn new police captain had closed all the after-hour joints in the ninth district, including the Hawaiian, and the Belle Haven on Belle Avenue, right off Vandeventer, where musicians used to sit in during the wee hours all the time. The corners had it that the Musician's, right down the street from the Club Riviera, was next to go too, and he halfway believed it because they had shut the little after-hour club in the back of the Riviera up tight. Jim, St. Louis sure was living up to its name of being a jive-time, country-assed town.

All his folks were glad to see him—at least the ones that got to see him. Helen was teaching Physical Ed in a high school down in Tennessee now, and his mother was out on Arsenal Street in Malcolm Bliss. He just couldn't get himself together long enough to go out there and see her. Argustus was married to Aunt Ida now and living over at her house, and Wilbur kept more company with some old sides of himself with Dirty Red, Ernie Fergens, and a fifth of gin, than he did with him, so that wasn't any fun. As far as his dad was concerned, they never talked much together about anything anyway so Raymond wasn't sorry when it became time for him to report for work at the post office.

Right after his dad left the doorbell rang.

"Hey, baby, long time no see."

"Jerome?"

"Heard you were in town man, thought I'd breeze by."

"Come on inside, man."

"Naw, man. You got time for a little spin, ain't you?"

"Well, yeh, man, I guess so. Just a minute. Let me get my coat."

Jerome had a brand new Coupe De Ville green and white convertible Cadillac.

"Hey, baby, what you been putting down?" Raymond wanted to know.

"Wait til you see who's in the short, man."

"Hi, Raymond."

"Jetan?"

"Hey man, I guess you heard Frankie Boy got wasted in Korea?"

"Naw, man, I didn't know."

"Yeh, drowned in one of them flash floods. You know that bastard never did learn how to swim."

"Aw, yeh? That's tough," Raymond said.

"Oh, I dunno," Jerome said. "His family got ten grand out the deal. He never would of been worth that much to nobody alive."

"Good to see you, Jetan."

"Yeh, Raymond, that's what I was thinking."

Jetan handed him a Jay, inside the car, as Jerome pulled off from the curb. They passed it back and forth between the three of them.

"Whatever happened to Lobo?"

"He's still up, man. He writes to me sometimes. He asks about you. But I tell him I don't never dig you. I'm working on trying to spring him loose, but it's a tough titty to nurse, you know how that is."

"Yeh, I dig," Raymond said.

"What have you been doing with yourself these last few years?" Jetan wanted to know.

"Same ole thing. You?"

She shrugged. "I've been making it." She took a deep drag, put the joint out and cocktailed the roach in a cigarette.

Jerome rounded a corner and Jetan's knee banged into Raymond's. She took a deep drag and passed him the cigarette. She didn't take her knee away.

Raymond took a deep drag and fireflies started darting through his head. "Um, Jack, this is some boss weed."

"Three X," Jerome said. "The toughest vaughns in town. You know some studs in the band want to cop a can or so, let me know."

"Okay, baby, I'll do that. That shouldn't be too hard to swing."

Raymond took a couple of hits and passed the stick to Jerome. "Yeh, man, you done really got into something these days, ain't you. Cadillac car, hundred-dollar suits, Knox Twenty hats, thirty-five dollar shoes. Church's ain't they?"

"Yeh, man, anything cheaper hurts my feet."

Jerome passed the roach to Jetan. "Um, man I'm sailing," he said.

Raymond got a couple hits and handed the cigarette to Jerome. "Here man, catch up with me," he said. "Sailing hell, man, I'm flying."

"You've changed," Jetan said.

"Huh, baby, how you mean?" Raymond said.

Jetan shrugged. "Oh, I dunno," she said. "Just changed, that's all." Then she wiggled the leg, that was against him, up and down. "But that's all right, I've changed too. I guess that makes us even."

Jerome handed over another joint. Raymond fired up. He was past sailing, he was past flying, he was blind. "Not quite, baby, not quite," he said, passing her the sweet-tasting joy stick.

23

. . . well, ain't nobody worried, and ain't nobody crying . . .

HER NIPPLES WERE ripened, maroon tips of huge golden berries and the way he held her breasts made them dangle in the palms of his hands. She gave him no peace, no rest. They slept together the whole two weeks the band was in St. Louis and cities on the East Side. She made love to him as though every minute was their last and she wanted to hold on to each second forever. She was as much at ease around him naked as he was around her with clothes on and they spent many a morning watching dawn creep up and ravish the sky through the half-drawn blinds of a hotel room, filled with the pungent odor of marijuana and the whining squeak of a bed. They watched each dawn, with their bodies interlocked like bunched-together zebra skin, and when the band pulled out, for a tour through the rest of the West, she cried.

Once they got away from St. Louis she haunted every waking moment. She burned him in his sleep. She gave him a five-ton monkey on his back which only she could take away. She hooked him, she had him snakebit, and all he could think about was getting back so she could give him another fix. All through Oklahoma City he was that way, all through New Orleans, all through L.A. San Francisco didn't cool him off and Portland, Washington, only made it worse. He spent his days longing to get back to St. Louis, in the "Show Me" state of Missouri.

Three months later they did get back, and when they did he didn't waste any time. He went busting down to her job on 12th and Spruce at the Army Transportation Corps.

"Raymond Douglas, my goodness. I can't leave now, I'll get fired."

"Tell them you quit."

"Raymond Douglas what's wrong with you?"

"Come on, I don't have much time. We're just passing through. We're leaving out of here tonight."

"But I'll lose my job."

"Who needs it?"

"Why I do!"

"Not where you're going. Come on," he told her.

You had to wait three days before you could get married in St. Louis so they went to a little farm town about a hundred miles down the river. That night they played a concert at Kiel Auditorium. The next morning they were on the road toward New York.

Jetan was crazy about New York, the streets, the houses, the people, the smells, the excitement of show life. She didn't mind the traveling on the road and during a performance, whether at the Savoy, Birdland, or some small joint in the wee hours on the wayside, you couldn't tear her away. He couldn't have gotten himself a better wife if he had invented her in a dream.

They had a ball. They had a natural ball.

. . . uh-uh-uh-uh-uh. People that is how I feel . . .

THEN JETAN GOT pregnant. When she found out she really was pregnant she cursed like a sailor.

That kind of hurt his feelings.

"Well Raymond, damn. It ain't like I don't want your baby. I just don't want no babies period."

That didn't help the situation.

"Oh goddamn, all right, if you going to act that way about it I guess I'll just have to go through with it, I suppose."

"You suppose. What you mean you suppose!"

"Oh Raymond, what are we hollering at each other for? Raymond I'm just scared. I can't help it I'm scared."

"Scared? Of what?"

"Oh, nothing. I suppose. I'll have it. I'll have it if you want me to."

He couldn't sleep good after that. He felt guilty. Imagine feeling guilty about knocking up your own wife!

She started having trouble after her fourth month. Raymond got scared and suggested sending her home to stay with her mother until the baby came, but she wasn't for it.

"You trying to get rid of me, Mr. Douglas?"

"Get rid of you, you kidding?"

" 'Course I am, can't you tell?" she said, placing his hand on her stomach.

"You clown," Raymond said. He nibbled at her ear.

"Ummm, honey, don't do that. I guess I haven't been much fun for you lately?"

"Baby, you're the best thing that ever happened to me. And don't you ever forget that."

She moved her bare back against him and he put his other hand on her stomach.

"Honey, can I tell you something?"

"What?"

"Promise you won't get mad first."

"Okay."

"I didn't love you when we first got married," Jetan told him. He didn't say anything.

"Honey?"

"I heard you," Raymond said.

"But I did want to marry you though, ever since high school."

"Um-hum."

"Please don't be mad, hear? 'Cause I do love you now. I guess

154

before, I was just too wrapped up in myself to really care about anybody else. I wanted to marry somebody I figured would go places. I guess that's why I was so crazy about you."

"And Tack," Raymond said.

"Yeh, and Tack too. Why did you do that?"

"Do what?"

"Bring up Tack?"

"I dunno," Raymond said.

"Please don't bring that up again, Raymond, hear? Please?"

"I don't want to bring it up," Raymond said.

"You know I didn't have his baby?" Jetan said.

Raymond didn't say anything.

"You know what?"

"What?"

"I figured if you got me pregnant, you'd marry me."

"You did, huh?"

"Uh-huh. Then you had to go and get me pregnant when it wasn't even necessary."

She glanced at him. "I shouldn't have said that."

"It's all right."

"No, I shouldn't have said it, but I will have it, Raymond. You'll see. I'm going to give you a beautiful baby boy."

"You are, huh?"

"Uh-huh. Raymond?"

"What?"

"You know I use to be Jerome's girl too?"

"What's done is done," Raymond said. "I don't care about the past. All I care is that you're my girl now."

"I'm more than that, I'm your wife."

"Yeh, uh-huh. So just see that you stay that way."

"Aw Raymond, you're so crazy. I wouldn't keep us from having this baby for nothing in the world. Raymond, no matter what happens it was worth it. These last few months were worth everything. Raymond, my Raymond," she said.

Two months later she was gone. Two months, twenty-four hours, forty-five minutes, and three tenths of a second later, a huge doctor, at City Hospital, came out into the emergency ward and told him Jetan had died on the operating table giving birth to his son. The doctor scolded him for letting his wife take a chance on having a baby with her chances only one out of ten of surviving childbirth, after she'd had that abortion. The fat doctor droned on and on.

"Yeh, man, yeh, what about the baby?"

"The baby was dead too. I'm sorry, I know how you must feel," the doctor said.

"Do you?" Raymond said. He put his balled-up fists into action lighting a cigarette. Then he turned on his heel and strolled out of the hospital.

"Why, that son-of-a-bitch doesn't even care," the doctor said. The doctor shook his head. The anthropologists, and the sociologists could say what they wanted to, but those colored people just weren't human.

. . . well, sometimes I think I won't. Then again I think I will . . .

HE GOT HIGH and stayed that way. After a week went by, and he still hadn't come down, or gone to work, Bennie paid the train fare and shipped him home.

"Whenever you get yourself together come on back," Bennie said. "The first trumpet chair'll always be open."

Raymond got home and wouldn't speak to anybody. People spoke to him, but he didn't hear what they said. He got high and went out on Arsenal Street, but they wouldn't let him visit when he got there. They told him he was the root of his mama's problems and that his success in music had pushed her beyond the brink of reality. The officials out there trained their patient smiles on him and he felt like pushing their smug white faces through the concrete floor. They smiled those smiles at him and something at the base of his spine exploded the knowledge in the pit of his stomach that as long as his mother remained in Malcolm Bliss she would never recover, and that there was something more deadly than just his musical career pushing her beyond that brink.

He started spending his time down on the rat-infested streets of Biddle, and Madison, and Sheridan, and Jefferson, and Clark, and Dickson, and Franklin Avenue, and Laclede, where people-packed, grayish tenement flats sprawled from corner to corner, mile after mile, far as the eye could see; where soggy bags of garbage cluttered the hallways and roaches and falling plaster battled to cover the walls; where no day passed without the neighborhoods being jarred by the oh-oo-ah of a squad car's siren, where ragged men peddled their souls for a half shot of whisky, where two-dollar prostitutes walked all day drumming up a dollar's worth of trade and white cops patrolled the beat like the mighty Tarzan taking his kingly swing through the trees of the jungle.

All over downtown, all over Soulville, he found weed flowing like water. All over Soulville he found guys buying weed with their relief checks, and babes buying weed with their ADC checks, and Tarzan swinging through the trees scowling while the guys and the babes got high and sat back in their pads and laughed. All over Soulville he found people not working and making it. James Henry (the guy Lobo had stomped a corn on in the L'Ouverture School yard, over fifteen years ago) had a good thing going in that part of town. James had people out pushing smack for him. James provided protection for his pushers too. He had a rep for killing two guys for trying to stick up one of his pushers. Mickey was hooked and pushing for him now, and so was Fatblack, Raymond heard, and James had two three-and-a-half-story apartment houses and a black Lincoln Continental. James Henry tried to turn Raymond on some smack, but he wouldn't go for the action. "Naw, man, I just dig weed, you dig that?"

"Yeh, nigger, well anytime you change your mind, just let me know."

James Henry hadn't changed much. "Man, being a musician you must know plenty of studs who get splibbed."

"Aw yeh, man?"

"Yeh, you get me a few good customers I might make it worth your while."

"Aw yeh?"

"Yeh, nigger, that's what I said."

A year passed like that and he stayed in Soulville because that was where it was at. After while they started calling him Splib, because he stayed laid all the time, and the local musicians stopped asking him to sit in. One night, he was firing up in a gangway with a bunch of guys when fire engines started rolling down Franklin Avenue. A skinny old woman came running out the house, her short hair going in all directions. "Hey, y'all, hey!" she said.

The fire engines kept rolling. More fire engines sped by.

The old woman kept standing out there shouting. Finally, a fire chief pulled his little red car over beside her and stopped. "Yeh, yeh, lady. What's wrong?"

"Where the goddamn hell is y'all going this time of night making all that goddamn noise?" the old woman said.

"What?"

"Y'all don't cut out that goddamn racket I'ma call the police!"

She didn't, but they came around anyway.

"Hey, Jack, clean up. Here comes the man."

Reefers disappeared everywhere.

He was too greedy to stop in the middle of a good high. He took a couple of more long hits, then ate the roach while the man was looking. The smell of vaughns and urine in the gangway was strong enough to floor a horse. The man smiled at Raymond, ran a handkerchief over his mouth and took him down.

There was a gray-headed Soulville citizen, in ninth district police station when they got there, explaining to the baldheaded desk sergeant about a robbery attempt.

"He broke in my house Your Honor."

"Look lady, I ain't no judge, I told you that before."

"But, sir, he tried to rob me, but I didn't have but thirty-five cents."

"Look lady—"

"And I offered him that, but he got mad and wouldn't take it."

"Yeh, lady, like I explained to you before—"

"Then he hit me and ran out the house, and I fell over the rocking chair and bumped my head when I was trying to get to the phone to call you."

"Yeh, lady."

"Ain't y'all gone do nothing about it?"

"Look, will you please sit over there and wait until Sergeant Mason comes out here like I told you?"

"But what y'all gone do?"

"Lady, the sarge'll be out in a minute and you tell him what happened and he'll fill out the report and then—"

"Hi, Bill."

"Hello Johnny, what you got."

"I want to book this boy on suspicion of narcotics possession," the slim white plainclothes man said.

"Aw, yeh. Caught him with it on him, huh?"

"Your Honor, what's y'all—"

"Aw, lady please."

"Yeh, he ate it, but I picked up a few crumbs with my handkerchief," the plainclothes man said.

"I ain't gone leave here till y'all does something," the gray-haired lady said.

26

THE DAILY PAPERS didn't have much to say. The weekly press had a field day.

RAYMOND DOUGLAS ARRESTED ON DOPE CHARGE!
DOPE FIEND WIPED CLEAN BY FUZZ!
JAZZ STAR ARRESTED FOR BLOWING DOPE!

All over the country his name bounced around in headlines. If he could have had a record out on the jukeboxes then, he would have cleaned up.

Hosea had a fit. "Getting arrested on Twentieth and Franklin of all places."

"Yeh, Dad, okay. Let's hurry up and get it over with."

"For smoking dope!"

"Marijuana is not dope. That's propaganda the cigarette companies got passed into law so they could pass cancer around with their own products."

"What are you trying to do, go backwards? After all the sacrifices your mother and I made for you."

"Yeh, I suppose it would have been better if I got stopped out on Elmbank somewhere, in a Cadillac with the local president of the NAACP's daughter."

"Boy, this isn't funny, you can go to jail."

"So I can go to jail."

"What's the matter with you? You act like you're crazy."

"Aw Dad, get up. The world ain't gone come to no end just 'cause I got busted down on Twentieth and Franklin blowing some Mary Jane."

"Pretty soon, all the money you've saved'll be gone."

"Well, why don't you go on and say it? I'm a bum because I don't dig nothing but laying around all day getting high."

"Aw, Raymond, Raymond," Hosea said.

Part Three

'Round Midnight

. . . just because I'm in misery . . .

THEY HELD HIM in jail for three days, down in twelfth district where they had all kinds of ways of keeping people from getting away. They also did a pretty good job of keeping visitors from talking to the prisoners they held inside.

Two guys were in the cell with him.

"What they got you in for baby?" asked the tall slim guy. He had red conked hair and wore old, faded army fatigues, turned up a quarter of an inch on each leg in a neat cuff.

"Cat popped me while I was holding some rooney," Raymond said.

"Aw yeh, man?"

"Yeh."

"Yeh, that's a bitch," the other one said. He was a light-tan guy with wide shoulders and a good build that was beginning to go soft. "Man, all them cats on the narcotics squad gets high themselves."

"Yeh, that's what I heard," said the guy with the red conked hair.

"Yeh, man, when them cats popped my brother-in-law, with nineteen cans, they went into the bathroom, supposed to be looking for something and when they came out, Jim they was laid, man."

"Yeh, well, they know it ain't nothing wrong with smoking a little rooney."

"Aw yeh, man, you know they know rooney ain't habit forming.

They got to know it, man, with all them doctors and technicians and things they got to test them things."

"Why you think they went and got it outlawed then, man?"

"You got me man, 'lessn it was because they couldn't put no tax on it 'cause it grows so wild and everything."

The guy with the conk laughed. Over in the next cell a hillbilly started singing one of those down-home songs he had heard some brown guy do somewhere once.

"I ain't got nothing but the blues," the hillbilly sang in a high, quivering nasal twang.

"Man, get him," the conk-headed guy said.

"He got the blues, ain't that a bitch. How in the hell he figure he's got the blues. I guess he thinks just 'cause he's in jail that gives him the right to have the blues, or somptin?"

"Man, I ain't arguing with you."

"Aw man, them cats kill me with that stuff. We put the word *blues* in the language, but they don't want us to have nothing. Them studs is so way out they even want to take our misery and claim it as their own."

"Man, I told you I wasn't arguing with you."

"Yeh, man, them studs is a bitch, ain't they man?" the red-haired guy said to Raymond.

Raymond didn't answer.

They figured him for a weirdo and let it go at that.

Funny how jail did things to people; made them think seriously along channels they had never thought along before. Funny. The world was out there, but you couldn't reach it. People were going along doing a hundred insignificant things that suddenly became very important to you simply because they could do them and you couldn't. That alone was enough to bug a cat out of his sanity. Freedom was something, yeh, freedom was really something, that was why having brown skin and being what people referred to as a Negro could be such a drag at times. One of these days I'm going to be free, he thought. One of these days I'm going to be really free. Funny thoughts for a guy behind bars facing a jail sentence for something there shouldn't even be a law on. Yeh, funny.

They came and took the guy with the conk away to stand trial for being at a service station with a loaded rifle in his hands.

The next morning they took Raymond and the tan guy down for the line-up in a large police-filled room downstairs.

They walked you up on a platform and shone a hard light in your eyes so that you couldn't see anybody except the other guys up on stage in the line-up with you. Almost like playing up on stage in a band.

The audience cracked up when they were told Raymond had gotten arrested when they found a few grains of marijuana on his lips.

Raymond started thinking about Jetan. Jetan of the honey voice and the mellow body. Jetan who had brushed her thighs against him on so many nights, and who had said she loved him almost as though it were a confession. Jetan who had died having a baby for him. They asked him questions and he started thinking about Jetan. Jetan whom he would never see again, never speak to again, never love again. He started thinking about Jetan, something he hadn't let himself do since it had happened.

The police didn't know how to figure him. They thought he acted kind of funny. They took him up on another floor, in a little room, where two narcotics detectives told him they would let him go if he told them who his contact was and ratted on all the cats out there in the street who he knew got high.

That was funny too.

HIS CASE GOT thrown out of court for insufficient evidence and he rode the reefer binge two solid years and then his money gave out.

"See," Hosea told him. "I warned you, but you wouldn't listen. Now what you going to do?"

"Okay, man, you don't have to preach about it. I'll move."

"Quit acting cute and take a good look at yourself in the mirror over there on the wall," Hosea told him.

"Aw man, why you always gotta carry me through some changes?"

Hosea grabbed Raymond by the shoulders and spun him over to the mirror hanging over the white front-room mantelpiece. "Goddamn you, I said take a look," Hosea said.

"Aw baby, now you really taking me through some changes," Raymond said.

He tried to dodge his image in the mirror, but Hosea made him look. He was a long series of wrinkles from shoulders to the cuffs in his Ivy League pants. He was two months overdue for a cutting session with a barber. His shoes hadn't seen polish for so long that the leather had cracked open in spots and started peeling back.

He laughed, shrugging it off. "What you want me to do, put a tie on?" he said.

"And you got the gall to call yourself a man," Hosea said.

Raymond went up and knocked on Wilbur's door.

"Yeh, Sport? Come on in."

"Hey dig. Me and the old man are kind of on the outs so I'ma split so I won't have to be going through them changes if you know what I mean."

"Well, Cut, it's your life, but I wish you would change your mind."

"Naw, I should of made it a long time ago, really," Raymond said.

"Yeh, well, you know what I've been doing lately? Wait a minute, sit down, I'll show you."

Wilbur got his trumpet out of the case, stroked the golden sides for a second or two and then raised it to his lips with his left hand. When he did that Raymond did sit down. Wilbur began to play the tune he had written when he was in the Army. He played it slow and warm, with full mellow lip slurs and clean strokes from nimble fingers. Wilbur played the tune the way he had never played it before, the way no one had ever played it before and as he played Raymond listened in awe the way he used to listen to Argustus play when he was a little boy and his mother was away from home. All of the heartache, the frustration, loneliness, and bitterness of being away from a soulmate for all of these years came out of that horn and Raymond sat there gaping like an inexperienced adolescent getting the first detailed description on the lowdown of what sex was all about.

"Yeh, I guess I still need to practice a little more. Kind of hard getting used to playing with my left hand," Wilbur said.

"Naw Uncle Wilbur, you saying something man, you really saying something," Raymond said.

"Yeh, well I guess I got enough to say far as that goes."

"Yeh. Yeh, man you were burning."

"Yeh, well, I'm glad you liked it, Sport. I'll tell you why."

Wilbur hit on him to join up with him and form a group. "We'd have it made," Wilbur said, "you and me, since we've already been in the big time."

"Well, yeh, but I don't know," Raymond said.

"Yeh, okay. Just thought I'd mention it. I guess I really ain't ready yet, I could stand a lot more practice."

"Aw naw, man, it ain't you, it's me. I ain't even looked at my horn in two years," Raymond said. "Naw, Unk, you're saying something, fair saying something, but I'd only be a drag on a set with you."

"All you'd need would be a little practice to get your chops and your fingers back. If I can learn to play all over again with my left, I know damn well you can start all over again and make it too," Wilbur said.

"Yeh, well, probably so but, aw hell Wilbur, I don't know, I mean, well it seems like my soul dropped out through my stomach, you know, when that thing happened?"

"Yeh, I know."

"Yeh, and I ain't never been able to get it back," Raymond said. "I just ain't got nothing left to say on a horn no more."

"Sure you have, Cut, but sometimes it takes a long time to get it out," Wilbur said. He slapped Raymond on the back. "I dig what you're getting at, you know I was on a gin binge myself for over ten years. Ten hell-a-fied years," Wilbur said reminiscing.

Raymond looked at Wilbur, his eyes getting red. "I thought about straightening up a couple of times, but I dunno. I just can't seem to catch up with myself right now."

"You don't have to explain, Cut. You got any dough?"

Raymond said he hadn't.

Wilbur let him have seventy-five dollars. "That ought to hold you for a while," he said.

"I'll straighten you in a couple of months."

Wilbur brushed him off. "If you get busted down and need some more dough, don't be afraid to drop on by," he said.

"I wish I could of done that thing with you," Raymond said.

"Aw that's all right, Cut, that's all right. Maybe I'll start a group on my own one of these days. Yeh, maybe I will. You never can tell."

3

"**H**EY BABY," Jerome said, opening the door to his $110 a month apartment. He lived out west, on Cabanne and Goodefellow where mainly upper-middle-class white people lived. "What's up?"

"Thought I'd drop by and take care of a little business."

"Yeh, man, come on in."

Jerome gave him a five-can play for $55. Jerome turned on his $800 stereo combination record player and TV set and they got high on some bombers and dug some sides for a while. They had a lot to talk about. They hadn't seen each other since he had married Jetan and taken her off to New York.

They didn't talk about Jetan. They talked about everything, but Jetan. Jerome gave Raymond a lot of good advice on how to keep from getting busted out there on the streets, and an extra half can of grass on the house.

"What you gonna wrap the stuff in to deal it with?" Jerome wanted to know.

"Tinfoil."

"Yeh, all that's good," Jerome said. "You can throw that a hell of a lot further than you can grass wrapped in paper if the man comes along."

"Yeh, I'm hip."

"You dig that flick Pinky yet?"

"Naw, man."

"I'm going Sunday, you want to go?"

"Naw, man, I don't dig no flicks where you suppose to feel sorry for somebody whose greatest problem is trying to pass for white," Raymond said.

"Yeh, I'm hip, me neither, but that ain't why I asked you."

"You lost me, baby," Raymond said.

"I was just showing you how the signal worked," Jerome said.

"See when you wanna score you can call me up and invite me to a flick. And if I'm holding I'll tell you when to drop by. If I ain't I'll call you back when I am and invite you to a flick, you dig that?"

"Yeh, man, that's swinging."

"Yeh," Jerome said. He explained the whole operation to Raymond, how to ask for a pound of grass, or cans, just by mentioning the time that they were supposed to go to the show.

"Yeh, man, that's heavy. That's about as cool as you could ask for anything to be," Raymond said.

"It better be," Jerome told him. "Otherwise I won't be able to stay out here, and incidentally, man, I have a different signal for each cat I turn on, you dig that?"

"Yeh," Raymond said. "That makes sense."

"Yeh, man, and the signals change all the time," Jerome told him.

Once Raymond got back to the apartment he had rented for $12 a week, he packaged up some five-dollar packs which contained three full teaspoons of grass, and some two-dollar packs that contained three fourths of a teaspoonful. He broke down two cans of grass in packs that way and found a couple of good hiding places to put away his stash. He lit another bomber and lay back on the bed in the narrow cell-like bedroom and Jetan's face flared up in the tiny fiery head of the stick of tea. Then out of the smoldering ashes another head leaped up to haunt him, the face of the woman who had given up her sanity just as his wife had given up her life. He shuddered in spite of himself. Both of them had said they loved him.

4

YOU ALWAYS WALK the streets facing the traffic so the man can't pull up on you from behind, and you don't let anyone get next to you while you're walking, and you carry the rooney in your hand next to the fences and the bushes and the houses that you're passing by and if the man comes you ditch it before he gets to you and remember where you did so that you can come back and get it after he's gone. You watch for aerials on the tops of cars because that means it's the man even though POLICE might not be written on the doors and you use the side streets and the byways and keep off the main arteries where the man has his wolf pack of squad cars patrolling the battleground. You just keep moving, that's your secret; you move, you don't fool around, you make it as fast as you can and take care of business as soon as you can, only you walk at a normal pace because not to is to attract attention and attention is something you can do without. You keep moving and after a while it gets to be old hat with you, pressure becomes an everyday ordinary thing and besides it's not too different from what you've been accustomed to all your life anyway, the cops have been riding you all your life anyway, so what the hell the only difference is now they really have something to ride you for, only they don't know it, and that's the biggest joke of all.

Winter is strong on the city in frosty paint icing over on the slush-filled streets. The gangways on Franklin Avenue are yellow with urine. People bulge out the bars and crowd the corner taverns. Rhythm and blues music pours from the cruising Cadillacs, the barbecue stands, the poolrooms, the dingy, rat-packed rooming houses over the merchant shops. The corner boys gang up on the lampposts and the store-front churches shout out the news about sweet Jesus to the neighborhood of winos, crap shooters, junkies, prostitutes, policy slip runners, police and reefer pushers.

Business was good. Long lines haunted the sidewalks with dark faces around the Missouri State Employment division down on 16th and Locust. Dark faces crowded the ADC office downtown on Washington Avenue and kept the new sociology graduates in jobs.

Business was good. Friday and Saturday night meant slaughter in the streets and Homer G. Phillips Hospital was kept in a steady supply of butchered customers.

Business was booming. Raymond couldn't keep enough grass to get rid of.

"Hey Jerome," he would say. "You going to that card party next Sunday night?"

"Naw man, but why don't you make it by Friday? I'ma throw one myself."

"What time?"

"What time can you make it?"

"Around eight-thirty."

"Aw yeh, man that's cool."

And Raymond would go over and pick up his half pound of grass.

Business was rocketing. After a while he was telling Jerome it would take him an hour to get over to his pad. A bill and a dime for a whole pound, that's all it took; a bill and a dime, and he couldn't get hold of it fast enough. He bought himself a 1953 Plymouth to get around town with and paid for it in no time. He was getting to the point where he could get rid of a pound of grass a month and that meant at least $100 a week for his troubles; only money didn't move him, money made no difference to him one way or another. As long as he had enough to pay his room rent, grocery bill, what other few expenses he had, and some grass to smoke whenever he felt like getting high (which was all the time), he was satisfied. He was what they called a viper. He stayed stoned all the time. If he had been on alcohol they would have called him a lush.

One day he had just finished delivering some grass to ole Lorraine Jordan who used to live over on Rutger, but was now down in the projects with a house full of babies and no ole man, when he bumped into a guy, wearing a full beard all over his face, as he went down the corridor.

"Hey, Raymond! Ole Raymond Douglas, well I'll be damned."

"Teacher," Raymond said recognizing the voice. "Man, I didn't recognize you in that thing, you know?"

"You mean the beard?"

"Yeh."

"Where you going, man?"

"I was just about to make it home."

"Well, hell, man, if you ain't got nothing up why don't you stop down at 309? That's where my ole lady stays."

"Aw yeh?"

"Yeh," Teacher said. "Yeh, man, I got a little grass and we can put on some jams, talk about old times and get laid."

"Solid," Raymond said.

He followed Teacher down the hall.

"What you doing for yourself these days?" Teacher wanted to know.

"Not too much of anything," Raymond said.

"Aw yeh, man, me neither. I'm going to school out at St. Louis U. for the G.I. bill, but it's a drag really," Teacher said, "but I ain't got the bread to go to school in Africa so I guess it'll have to do."

Raymond looked at Teacher.

Teacher didn't crack a smile. "Hey baby, look who I run into out in the hall," Teacher said pushing open the door and going into a living room which had a gray fluffy rug on the floor and full drapes over the window to match.

A good-looking, light tan baby-faced woman, in her late twenties, looked up and broke into a smile.

"Well goodness gracious, Raymond Douglas."

"Inez."

"Boy I haven't seen you since grade school."

"Yeh, me neither."

"Inez told me y'all used to be tight in grade school," Teacher said.

"Aw Bruce it was just kid stuff that's all. Tell him, Raymond."

"That's it. After all that's what we were, kids," Raymond said.

"I used to have a hell of a crush on him, but he was scared to death of girls and so bashful he couldn't hardly talk," Inez said.

Teacher laughed. "Yeh, that sounds like old Raymond," he said.

Raymond laughed. "How you been making it, Inez?" he said.

"Oh I can't complain," Inez said, "and you?"

"Oh I'm making it."

"I heard about your wife. I was sorry to hear that."

"Yeh," Raymond said.

"You know I got a bone to pick with you," Inez said. "Just when I was bragging about going to school with you, all over town, you got out of the entertainment field."

Raymond shrugged. "Well you know how that is. It's just one of those things."

"And that thing you had with the police, that was funny as hell if it hadn't been so serious," Inez said.

"You really been keeping tabs on my man, ain't you?" Teacher said.

"Oh Bruce, really, why don't you go out and bring back some beer," Inez said.

"Wow, baby, the way you're coming on I think I might be better off sending Raymond off for the beer," Teacher said.

Inez cracked up. "Bruce, sometimes I just don't know what I'm going to do with you," she said.

Teacher started out for the beer. "Put some jams on and roll up some," he said. "I'll be right back."

"Whatever happened to that college freshman you were so stuck on?" Raymond asked Inez after Teacher had gone.

Inez's eyes misted up. "Naturally it didn't work out," she said. "We were married for five years. John's such a sweet guy really. He felt sorry for me so he took care of me. He still does. Everything you see in here he bought. Raymond," she said, "do me a favor?"

"What's that?"

"Don't tell Bruce about us."

"Aw that? You know I wouldn't do nothing like that," he said.

"Well, that *that* you're talking about would just about ruin everything between me and Bruce and I don't intend to let that happen. I've invested too much time, money, and sex on that guy to call things off now."

Raymond laughed. "Inez, I see you ain't changed none."

"What do you mean by that?"

"Nothing, you always were a gas," he said.

Teacher broke back in the door with a six-pack of Falstaff. "Hey, y'all ain't rolled the joints yet. What y'all been doing?"

"Talking about you," Inez said and winked at Raymond.

Teacher put some sides on the box and Raymond rolled up some joints from a matchbox Inez gave him.

They got high and listened to Miles Davis's album called *Walking*. They got out there and everything got real funny and they laughed until they couldn't see straight. They got laid and Teacher started talking that talk, the kind of talk the Muslims talked, only Teacher was much better at it. It turned out Teacher had been a prisoner of war in the Korean War. It turned out that once Teacher got high he was all mouth, all ideas, all convictions, and if you listened to him you would go away more than halfway convinced Teacher knew what he was talking about.

"Yeh, the stuff's gonna hit the fan in 1964," Teacher said. "China and Africa's gonna be right over here dead on Mr. Charlie's throat."

"Ooo, Teacher, I'm high," Inez said. "Don't you take advantage of me, hear?"

Raymond took the hint and went home.

5

WILBUR HAD RENTED a little place on Grand and Enright, and named it Wilbur Anderson's Golden Trumpet. There weren't many people in the place, but Wilbur didn't seem to be worried about it. He was togged down in a mean three-buttoned charcoal-brown suit with the Ivy League lapels and the horn strap around his neck was studded with diamonds. His name was up in lights that you could see a half block away and though both the bar and restaurant were small they were the plushest things members had seen around Soulville in a long, long time. Raymond, giving it the once-over, thought that the Golden Trumpet just might have a good chance of making it after all. It should, his uncle had sunk every dime he could scrape up into it and then had to go out and borrow some dough from a white guy he used to gig with when he was with Ernie Fergen in order to do it up right.

Argustus and Ida made Raymond come over and sit at their table.

Ida complimented him for looking as well as he did and bawled him out about never coming around to see them. Argustus asked him when the hell was he going to pick up his horn again. "I didn't learn you all them tricks for nothing, boy," he told him.

He felt uncomfortable as hell, sitting there high as hell, trying to hold down a family chit-chat with Argustus and Ida and listen to Wilbur blow all at the same time.

Every time he saw his uncle put the trumpet to his lips with his left hand and blow he felt like everything in the pit of his stomach was shaking loose. He sat silently listening to Wilbur play what it was like to be really blue, down-under-the-bottom-topside-up blue, like only a man being horribly misused by his country could possibly understand, and in his mind's eye he heard Teacher's booming bass voice, "Yeh, man I wear a beard as a sign of protest, just like the corner boys do, you dig. See man, the corner boys are already anti-social anyway so naturally they'd be among the first to start wearing beards. It's hard to call a man a boy when he's wearing a beard, and the day you see most spooks walking around sporting beards, look out, Jack, look out."

"You be sure you come by and see us soon now, you hear?" Ida was saying.

Unconsciously Raymond's hand rose up from the table and began stroking the flesh of his own smooth, closely shaven chin.

"WE'VE GOT ALL KIND of ancestors," Teacher told him.

"Man we got Irish, French, Dago, Japanese, Chinese, and a whole lot of other kind of folks in us besides African and anybody that says we ain't is a goddamn liar."

"Um, Teacher this stuff makes you feel good," Inez said taking a deep drag off the bomber Raymond had given her. "It feels almost as good as making love, only in a different way."

"Man, our people are something different all right, and that ain't no lie," Teacher said. "That's why everybody's scared of us."

Raymond said he supposed Teacher had a point.

"You damn right I got a point. You know anybody over here that ain't a bastard? Name one boot over here, man, that ain't got bastard blood in him; name one."

Raymond didn't argue with him.

"Yeh, man, we're all bastards. Every living mother-loving one of us is got that grey-boy blood in us, and all we got to do is to look down the family tree long enough to find out that's true. The gray boy had a field day with our women during slavery," Teacher said.

"Yeh, man, I guess you're right," Raymond said.

"You guess? Man, what's there to guess about? But I'ma tell you something, man. We ain't got time to be worrying about none of them races really. See we ain't really a race, man, we're a people, but if we were a race I'd rather be a black man than a white man any day, 'cause Jim, let me tell you, that gray boy's in a world of trouble."

"Aw yeh, man?"

"Yeh, man," Teacher said.

"That's why this beatnik movement is taking over now," Inez said getting into the conversation. "The white man knows his time has run out and he's gonna lose everything, maybe even his life if he's not mighty careful."

"Damn right," Teacher said. "That's why it's such a drag to hear boots running around talking 'bout they're beatniks. Man, some of our folks are out of sight. They want to integrate themselves into everything, even the white man's headaches."

Raymond settled back on the couch and got high listening to Teacher and Inez talk that talk. After a while they had him talking that talk too.

"Yeh, those cats even got the nerve to want to claim they invented jazz," Raymond said, "and jazz ain't their story. Jazz is the story of the black men being messed around so bad by the white man that if he could he'd lay down and die from the blues but his soul won't let him do it."

"Yeh, man," Teacher said. "Jazz is the story of the black man being mongrelized, physically, spiritually, and culturally."

"Man, you sure using a lot of big words these days, you know that?" Raymond said.

"Yeh, well I'm a college man now, man."

They got high as hell on some good vaughns that had them laughing after everything they dug in the conversation.

"Yeh man a boot running around claiming he's beat is about

as far off base as a gray boy running around talking 'bout he's got the blues," Teacher said.

"Yeh, man, I'm hip to that," Raymond said.

"Yeh, man, a boot ain't never had enough of nothing to know how it feels to lose everything and a gray boy ain't never lived under the social conditions to know what the blues is all about."

"Yeh, beatnik is a hell of a name for a stud who's supposed to be *down,* ain't it?" Raymond said.

"I'm hip. It's a riot really."

They laughed.

"Oh, I don't know. I think it's a beautiful description of a hell of a mistake," Inez said.

"How you mean, baby," Teacher said.

"Well, all a beatnik is is a white man who sees he's about to lose everything and attempts to go Negro in order to lessen the shock."

Teacher laughed. "Yeh, that's it," he said.

Raymond looked at Inez. He could see she was serious. Ole Teacher was really something to get a babe like Inez to start talking that kind of talk. Well, she said she was going to get him, and with the stuff she was using on him he didn't see how she could lose. Ole Teacher didn't know it, but he was about to get himself a wife.

"Beatnik is a good description," Inez said. "You know—beat Nick. Now it's really a mistake when you beat Santa Claus."

Teacher burst out laughing. "Yeh, that's what the Middle East calls Uncle Sam," he said. "And if you think they ain't whipping a game on him, Jim you just ain't bright enough to be alive."

Raymond lit another joint, sucked in the smoke, held it, climbed up higher on the peace clouds of the poignant-smelling Mexican brand cigarette.

"Yeh," Teacher told him, "those people are out of sight. They tell you right in their history books what's happening with them. If them southern crackers would give them other gray cats a break they might have a chance, but what the hell, you can't expect the descendants of a bunch of whores, thieves, and gangsters to act too much different from their parents."

181

"What do you mean?" Raymond said.

"Aw hell, man, don't go to Nut City on me now, Jack. You know damn well the South was settled by a bunch of jailbirds that England sent over here so they wouldn't have to be bothered with 'em. Man, that's why you got so much violence in the South, and the West too, man."

"Aw I don't know," Raymond said.

"Look man, any time some cats can move in and steal a whole country from somebody the way these studs did the Indians and then commit genocide against whole nations, which they also did against them same Indians, and then enslave the black man, and muscle in and take over the rest of the world in a fit of piracy, which they called imperialism, and then sit back and expect everybody to love 'em, they got to be a bitch. Man, violence is those people's nature. That's why they're so goddamn good at it."

"Aw I don't know," Raymond said.

"Man, I thought you'd done got hip to 'em by now, baby," Teacher said, "but I see you're still just a jive-time square."

Teacher and Lobo were true cousins, Raymond realized. Teacher used words the way Lobo used his fists. Teacher gave Raymond a pile of books to read, works by A. J. Rogers, Roi Ottley, Du Bois, William Franklin Frazier, Paul Robeson, James Weldon Johnson, and a lot of other guys.

Raymond spent weeks sitting in at home at his crib reading. A funny thing happened after that. When he got through he started letting his beard grow.

7

"**H**EY BABY."

"Hey, Jerome," Raymond said answering the phone. "What's up?"

"Lobo's getting out the joint next Thursday."

"Aw yeh, man?"

"Yeh," Jerome said. "I didn't want to say nothing about it until I was sure I could spring him."

"Yeh, that's swinging," Raymond said.

"Yeh, my man got in office up in Jefferson City," Jerome said, "so I was able to make a little deal. It cost me a nice little taste of change, but what the hell, I figure the stud would of done the same for me."

"Yeh," Raymond said.

"Yeh, man, why don't you drop over by the pad next Thursday night. I'm throwing one to celebrate."

"Crazy," Raymond said. "I'll be there."

There were a lot of people at the party whom Raymond hadn't seen in a long time. Mickey and Fatblack, and Snake who was a corporal on the police force these days. Snake told him Weasel was one of the guys who had gotten wasted trying to stick up one of James Henry's pushers last year. Snake said the police force was the best gig he could get, after being an MP in the Army. He laughed about it. "Can you imagine a stud like me, who used to be one of the baddest mammy-tapping gangleaders in this jive-time town, now trying to uphold the law in this raggedy, jive-ass city?"

Raymond had to admit he couldn't imagine it.

Inez and Lorraine, who had come with Raymond, began talking about ole times.

Teacher was talking to Jerome and Mickey. "Yeh, man, I sure

was a jive-time stud in those days. Can you even imagine somebody ratting on their own cousin the way I did Lobo?"

"Yeh, man, that wasn't cool," Jerome said.

"Fair wasn't," Mickey agreed.

"Yeh, man, I was so lame, it makes me sick to even think about it," Teacher said. "But man, I didn't know. Man, I was dead in those days if you know what I mean? If I had known then what I know now, I wouldn't of never pulled no stunt like that on Lobo, or you either, Raymond. See—I wasn't hip to myself, I didn't know nothing 'bout my people's history then. If I had I would of been cool, I would of stuck with you man, till the end."

"Yeh, sure you would of, man. Sure you would of."

"Aw man, you don't have to act like that about it. You did get even, you know."

"Yeh," Raymond said, thinking back to the scene in that little Deer Street room with the cops. "Yeh, I damn sure did."

"Hey, everybody, y'all help y'all self to this rooney." Jerome had a whole can of grass out on the table. "I don't wanna see nobody going home until it's all gone."

"Aw, Jerome, you're kidding," Lorraine said.

"You heard the man, smoke up," Snake said, "and I better not catch nobody taking some home with him, that's an automatic bust," he said, " 'cause see, that's stealing."

Everybody laughed. Inez and Jerome's girl, Sue, got off in a corner and discussed strategy while Lorraine kept a cool and casual eye out for Lobo to come busting through the door.

They played the album 'Round Midnight by Miles Davis.

Sue claimed she had gone to high school in East St. Louis with Miles Davis.

Lorraine and Inez said they had gone to school with Raymond Douglas.

They played some Bennie Williams sides with Raymond Douglas taking some long solos. Everybody told him how much they dug his playing on those sides.

They played "Green Haze" and "No Smoke" and "Bag's

Groove" with their classic Miles Davis solos. Then Lobo walked in the door.

Lobo was six-three and 220 pounds. Every ounce of Lobo was muscle. He had his hair cut right down next to his scalp, Muslim style, and a scowl was riding his forehead like the world had treated him wrong.

"My man!"

"Hey, Lobo!"

A half smile crawled up the right side of Lobo's face. "What you studs got to drink in this place?" he said. "Man, after twelve years in stir, I'm thirsty."

That cracked the party up.

"What's so funny, man? Don't tell me don't none of you cats get high no more?"

That really cracked them up.

"Say man, y'all shouldn't do that, that ain't cool," Teacher said.

"Look who's talking."

"Naw man, 'stead of acting like he's a big joke or something, you should be welcoming him home like a big-time war hero, 'cause actually that's what he is."

"Man, let me have a hit off that reefer you smoking," Snake said.

"Naw, man," Jerome said. "We glad to see you back, Lobo, you know that, it's just that what you said was kind of funny, man."

"A riot really," Fatblack said.

"Yeh, man, it was a gas. How you been doing, Lobo?"

"Hey, Raymond, what's been happening?"

"Naw, man, you can't explain it away like that," Teacher said. "I still say it wasn't cool. Hell, this cat's done knocked off one of the common enemies of all mankind and—"

"Man, where the hell you pick up on this jive-time stud from?" Snake wanted to know.

Jerome shrugged like it was beyond him.

"Yeh, man, that's the way it is. We live in an underground. They white and they say we black, but hybrid is what they mean, and the oppressors, or the white folks as we call them, naturally don't want us to know it, 'cause hell, they know if we did, we'd be fighting 'em like hell, just like those conquered people did the Nazis in Europe when Hitler was occupying everything."

"Man, this cat's been smoking too much of that dope," Fatblack said.

"Yeh, man, you better cut down some," Snake said.

"Yeh, man, what's this with your cuzz?" Jerome asked Lobo.

"Man, you asking me? I been locked up in stir for the last twelve years. How the hell you expect me to know?" Lobo had dreamed of going upside Teacher's head ever since he had gotten arrested, messing him up, really doing him in, but this cat with the beard, doing the talking here, was a stranger to him, somebody he didn't know. What the hell had gotten into Teacher anyway?

"Man, you better watch who you talk that talk to," Snake told Teacher. "The wrong studs hear you talking like that and you're gone for ninety-nine years and one dark day with the whole set of keys to the jail thrown away."

"Yeh, man, well the best thing for those people to do is to leave me alone, really. In fact they'd be better off getting up off of all of us, 'cause actually man we're their salvation." Teacher's eyes skipped back and forth on everybody in the room. "We're the ofay's savior, for the next four thousand years anyway," he said. "The only chance them cats got to make it is by integrating with us so-called colored folks, only they ain't got sense enough to know that and that's why so damn many of 'em are gonna get wiped clean off the face of the earth."

"Hey man, what is this, a tea party?" Lobo wanted to know.

"Yeh," Jerome said. "Have a stick."

"No thanks," Lobo said looking at Teacher. "Man, if vaughns makes you act like that I think I'd better leave it alone."

"Every boot in the country should be smoking it," Teacher said. "Pot makes you think, and once you start thinking it's goodbye Mr. Charlie. That's why the gray boy don't want you smoking it," Teacher said.

That kind of put a damper on the evening as far as the party was concerned anyway.

Raymond looked at Teacher. Even at a party he had to talk that talk. Man, what was with this cat anyway?

LOBO'S MOTHER WANTED HIM to stay at home with her, but he moved in with Raymond. He didn't want to have nothing to do with his mama. Lobo remembered hearing too many bill collectors in the bedroom with his mother, too many insurance collectors, too many rent men. The people who took the money out of the neighborhood were always white. Lobo had seen too many of them coming into his house, and that was why even now, every time a white man smiled at him it made him mad. So he moved in with Raymond.

His mother said he was ungrateful. His mother said she had kept him from going to the gas chamber by writing to President Roosevelt and getting him to stop the execution. Well, maybe she had, he couldn't tell one way or another since it had all been done behind scenes and kept out of the newspapers because the President didn't want nothing to get out that might hurt the war effort, or so his mother said. Well damn that. Damn what she had done for him when he was in jail, he wasn't going to stay in that house with her. There were too many wrong kind of memories there.

So he stayed with Raymond out on Taylor Avenue. He stayed with Raymond and started messing around with Lorraine Jordan again. He made it with Lorraine every chance he could. Twelve years without a woman was a long time.

Lorraine got Lobo started on smoking grass, and Lobo would

always make sure he was good and high before he went in to talk to his probation officer. The patrol officer was something, always at him to get a job and all that kind of stuff.

He spent a lot of time over at Inez's with Raymond and his cousin Teacher. Teacher was a gas, always talking that talk, only unlike before, Lobo dug what he was saying these days.

"Man you keep talking that talk they gone send you away from here."

"Well, I still say the next full-scale war we have on this planet is gonna be a race war," Teacher told him.

"Aw what makes you so sure?"

"You just wait, you'll see," Teacher said. "The United States and Russia are gonna be partners when the deal goes down, almost all the white nations are, and they're all going down before the Chinese-African onslaught too, baby, you better believe it they are."

"Yeh, well, where the hell do we fit into the scheme of things if all what you're saying is true?" Raymond wanted to know.

"That's a good question, Jim, that's a damn good question. That's what the hell I'd like to know," Teacher said frowning.

"Man, where you come up with this jive you preaching?" Lobo asked him. "You always did make out like you knew so much about everything and it always turned out you didn't know nothing."

"Here," Teacher said, practically throwing books at Lobo. "Use your brain for a change, man. Do a little reading; everything that's going to happen is right before your eyes. Here man, read these."

"Hey," Inez said, taking back some of the books Teacher was laying on Lobo. "You'll have to wait for these, I haven't finished them yet."

"And while you're at it, check the Bible," Teacher said. Teacher picked up a large reference Bible and started marking out passages for Lobo. "Look here man, Jesus was a black man, with eyes of fire, hair like wool, and feet like burnt brass, and Moses man, that stud was out of sight. Here man," he said handing the Bible to Lobo, "read this, it's all there."

9

"**H**EY, RAYMOND, look here," Lobo said one day. "Remember that band we used to always talk about starting when we were kids?"

"Yeh," Raymond said. "Yeh, that was something."

"Yeh," Lobo said, "so guess what? I was the best stud around the joint when it came to singing."

"Aw yeh?"

"Yeh. I won so many talent shows they stopped letting me participate. They said it was unfair to the others, how about that?"

"Yeh, well, that sounds pretty good, Lobo."

"I'm hip, what do you say to you and me getting together now and starting one?" Lobo said.

"Starting what?"

"A band," Lobo said. "What you think I been talking about all this time, man?"

"Aw yeh, well, I done retired from show business, man."

"Yeh, that's what Jerome was telling me. He said you gave it up right after your wife—what's her name?"

"Jetan."

"Yeh, that's it. I knew it was a funny name, but I couldn't remember what it was for sure. Anyway he said you got out of show business right after she died," Lobo said. "That's right, ain't it?"

"Yeh, I suppose so," Raymond said. "What else did Jerome tell you about me?"

"Nothing much," Lobo shrugged, "except you were what everybody in the trade referred to as a viper these days."

"What'd he mean by that?"

"A viper is the same thing on tea that a drunkard is on alcohol," Raymond said.

"Aw yeh, man, well why he wanna say something like that about you, I wonder?"

"I don't know," Raymond said. "Maybe he said it just because it happened to be true."

"Yeh, well, anyway it was a good idea," Lobo said.

"What was?"

"The idea about the band, man."

"Aw yeh. Yeh, man, I guess it was," Raymond said.

Lobo scouted out a cigarette butt in the ash tray, shook loose some tobacco in some cigarette paper and fixed himself a roll-your-own. He also split his match in sections so he could get more than one light off it, even though matches and cigarettes were plentiful for him these days. He did these things unconsciously. Some habits you picked up in stir were hard to break.

One day Raymond came home excited. "Hey man, you remember that cop, Pezzarus?"

"Naw. I don't know no cop by that name."

"Yes you do, man. You know that cat who was the partner of that stud you wasted?"

"Aw, him," Lobo said. "Yeh, what about him?"

"He almost blew Fatblack's head off while he was trying to hold up a filling station," Raymond said.

"No kidding?"

"Yeh," Raymond said. "Man, they don't know whether the stud's gonna make it through or not."

"Man, the bims around this mammy-tapping town is something, ain't they?"

"Yeh," Raymond said. " 'Course Fatblack should of have had more sense than to be messing around out there trying to stick up an ole jive-time filling station anyway," Raymond said.

"I'm hip," Lobo said. "That's what I keep trying to drum into Mickey's head, but it don't do no good."

"Yeh," Raymond said, "but let me tell you the rest. Snake said Pezzarus is getting promoted to the narcotics division so you know what that means."

"No kidding?"

"Yeh, so one time or another we'll probably meet up again."

"Yeh, that's okay too."

"Aw, I ain't worrying about him," Raymond said. "Aw yeh, there's something else I forgot to tell you. Snake said the cat recommended that the police department train dogs to use in boot neighborhoods."

"No kidding?"

"Yeh, that's what he said. He said the police board is taking it under consideration too, because of all the trouble ofays is having trying to collect bills from folks down in the projects."

"What kind of trouble, man?"

"Aw, cats been jumping on 'em and hanging 'em in the corridors and the elevators," Raymond said.

"So they gonna use dogs, huh?"

"Well, man, all I know is they thinking about it."

"You know what, man?"

"Naw, man, what?"

"Maybe my cousin Teacher ain't so crazy after all, man," Lobo said.

OBO DROPPED BY the Golden Trumpet early one Friday morning when there was a jam session going on in full swing. He just walked up on the stand while they were swinging "Going to Chicago Blues," grabbed the microphone and started belting out that tune. The musicians dropped a few licks, but they recovered after a spell and since it was sounding all right they continued to play.

Lobo brought the house down. That's how he got a singing-waiter gig from Wilbur and the probation officer off his back.

11

S TRANGE MUSIC WAS FLOATING from the radio. Hot, pulsating music with a jungle drive that painted leaping pictures of train-yard fires whipped along by the blowing breeze of a passing train whistle. Strange music floated from the radio gyrating behind a trumpet solo from the throat of a performer who played like he had a blues-colored soul.

Mae blinked her eyes over in the corner where she was sitting quietly at a table. The music did something to her. The music made her heart stop beating. The music sent shivers down her spine.

"That great classic trumpet solo you heard, in 'Big City Blues,' was taken by St. Louis's own Raymond Douglas, when he was with the great Bennie Williams aggregation," Mae heard the disc jockey say. "Raymond, as you know, was once a pretty influential figure in the jazz world until a few years ago when he sank into obscurity under mysterious circumstances that have never been completely revealed to the public."

Mae screamed, and as she screamed the room suddenly came crashing into focus before her eyes. She thought she was in a hospital, because that's where they had taken her after she became real sick at home and the women in the room all were wearing gowns of the type which were worn in hospitals, only they were so strange-looking and odd-acting that she became frightened and screamed, at least that was what she thought. She got hold of herself and cut the scream off. She looked around and saw a large female attendant sitting over by the door. Since when did Homer Phillips start hiring white nurses, she wondered? She wondered how many days she had been in the hospital. She felt all right now. She tried standing up and felt she was pretty strong. She decided to go over and ask the nurse when they were going to let her go home, and as she walked by the door she caught a glimpse of her image in the glass.

She stepped back, thinking an old wrinkled-faced, gray-haired woman, with flecks of spittle around the corner of her mouth, was coming in the door, but when she stepped back the figure in the glass stepped back also. She threw her hand up and a long bony hand shot out before the face of the woman in the door.

"Oh Lord," she said. "Oh no, not that. Oh Lord, please don't let it be that," but it was and she knew it was and the tears began to trickle down her cheeks.

"Now Mae Douglas, don't you start that," the attendant said. "You promised you were going to be a good girl today and I see you're working yourself up to throw another fit."

The tears ran.

"Now honey, you stop that, or I'll have to call Dr. Carson, and you know what that means, you'll have to go and take another shock treatment. Now you don't want that to happen, do you?"

Mae backed away from the attendant and ran over into a corner by herself away from the others, as far away as she could get from all the others. She sat down on the floor in a corner and let the tears run until they couldn't run anymore and when she got through doing that she looked around for something, anything that you could do damage with, and when she could find nothing, she pushed her tongue back into her throat, as far as she could, and swallowed it.

12

THE WHOLE FAMILY was there for the funeral—Hosea's folks and Argustus's too.

Helen, back from Tennessee with Jimmy, couldn't stand to look at Mae, and Raymond didn't blame her one bit. What was in that casket even turned his stomach and he was high as hell when he got there.

Hosea's eyes were so red they glowed like smoldering coals. Dad really loved Mama, he realized. The impact of the knowledge laid him low. Here he had been acting like he had been the only man on this planet Earth to ever lose a woman he loved and his old man had been suffering through the same thing for years and never mentioning a word about it, and not only that but he had continued going through the same daily routine, going to work and everything just as though nothing had happened. He was a fool. He was a damn fool to behave the way he had after losing Jetan. He felt very close to his old man, and looking around in the church he saw others in that room who had lost love and suffered too, just like he had. There was his Grandpa Argustus, who had lost his woman in a violent manner that never had been satisfactorily explained to him, and what about Wilbur and his Marsha?

"Raymond," Helen told him. "I wish you'd do me a favor. It'll probably be years before we see each other again, but I wish you'd do something for me, I really do."

Raymond nodded, he knew what she was going to say.

"You had such wonderful dreams when we were kids, remember?"

He nodded.

"I had dreams too. They may not have been as big as yours, Raymond, but to me they were just as important. I was going to be the first girl to win four gold medals in the Olympics, I was going to show Jesse Owens and everybody else what we women could do, and I was going to be famous and important, and make a lot of money because everybody thought so much of me. Oh believe me, Raymond I had dreams. I really had dreams. Everybody has dreams, Raymond. Even your kid sister."

He squeezed her arm.

"But dreams don't always come true; dreams seldom ever come true the way you plan them. That's what we all find out sooner or later when we grow up, and if we don't find out, Raymond, then we never grow up, you know what I mean?"

"Yeh, sis, I'm hip to it," Raymond said.

"Then let Jetan go. She's dead, just like Mama is dead now . . ." Her voice broke. "Let her go, Raymond; please let her go before it's too late."

Helen started crying and Jimmy pulled her to his shoulder.

"Hi, Raymond?"

"Hi, Jimmy, how you been making it, man?"

"Aw the town is small, but I like coaching high school track and with Helen teaching there too we've been making it okay."

"When you going to have some kids?"

"When we can afford 'em."

Raymond smiled, and tapped Jimmy on the shoulder with his balled-up fist. "Man, you misuse my sister I'ma bust your eyeball," he said grinning.

Jimmy smiled and slapped Raymond on the shoulder. Raymond had to get out of there, his eyes were on fire too.

The day after the funeral he went by and saw Argustus and Ida over on Sarah Street.

Ida cried and blew her nose when he told her what he was going to do. "The good Lawd's done finally answered my prayers," Ida said. "I always did tell your granddad you were a better musician than he and Wilbur put together on any day of the week."

Argustus slapped Raymond on the back. Argustus blew his nose too.

Raymond finally managed to get himself to go over and talk to his old man on Cora Avenue.

Hosea's eyes got red as fire again and Wilbur wanted him to come down to his club and celebrate.

"Not now," Raymond told him shaking his head. "Give me some time to get myself together."

Wilbur's eyes got red as fire too. "That's cool enough, Sport," he said. "Any time is all right with me."

Raymond's eyes caught fire, but he didn't feel bad; he felt like he was going to be able to straighten up and walk like a man for the first time in his life.

13

HE PRACTICED HARD for three months, running scales to build up his chops and limber his fingers. He practiced long, hard, and incessantly. His mouth ached at night, his jaws burned, his lungs felt like they were going to explode.

He punished his body because he was in too big a hurry to slow down to the pace it could tolerate. He only stopped when he reached the point where to continue would ruin his lips for playing a horn forever, and the three-room apartment was filled with the sound of a golden-throated trumpet.

The first thing he noticed right away was his change in style. He played like somebody he had never heard before. He had to cut down on vaughns because you couldn't practice well if you stayed high all day, and all of his spare time, when he wasn't pushing grass, he was practicing. Six months went by that way before that misty Friday morning, early in the spring of '59, when he walked into Wilbur's with his horn and mounted the stand to take his turn during a jam session.

The note he played shocked the place, and the local cats on the stand put him down. Some of them even got down off the stand, refusing to play with him as though he was violating the horn, or something.

"Yeh, man, I can't cut no groove like that."

"Naw, man, that's what comes from staying stoned all the time."

"Yeh, Jim, might of known old Splib was gonna put some stuff in the game."

"Don't worry about it," Wilbur told him afterwards. "You were great."

"You really think so?"

"You ever known me to bullskate you about your playing?"

Raymond had to admit he hadn't.

Lobo thought he was great too. Lobo hit on him about his idea of forming a band again. "I sure would like to sing some lyrics to some of them notes you were playing," Lobo said.

Raymond went over to Inez's and told Teacher about it.

"Yeh, well I'd keep right on developing along those lines if I were you," Teacher said.

"But, do you think the public'll go for it?"

"Aw the hell with the public. Don't worry about them. They go for what they figure it's supposed to be cool to go for."

"Yeh, man, but, aw I don't know," Raymond said.

"Look man, tell me this, can you play any other way?"

"Naw, I guess not, now that you mention it."

"Then that's it, don't worry about it, man. Keep working and perfect it. Everything'll turn out fine."

"How you figure that?" Raymond wanted to know.

"Well, see, man, in this world what you got to do to be a success is find out what makes a thing behave the way it does, why, and apply the principle. Now from what you just told me, I'd say you've got two thirds of that formula already licked."

THE NEWS FLOWED like reefer smoke over Soulville.

"Hey man, ole Splib's got a group going!"

"Splib?"

"Yeh, man, you know Splib; ole Raymond Douglas."

"Aw yeh man, what's he saying?"

"Man he's something else."

"No kidding, man; his group's cooking, huh?"

"Man, sizzling is more like it."

"Hard enough to brown, man?"

"Man, that's what I been standing here trying to run down to you."

"No kidding, man, I'ma have to make it down to dig that cat."

And they did make it down. They made it down in droves. They made the Golden Trumpet the place to go around town. Winter set in. Cold, limpid-sun days set against the dull slate sky. Snowstorms blanketed the coats of police dogs patrolling the foot of the projects. Squad cars convened on unwary brown-skin drivers like a wolf pack of white Nazi subs with their red periscopes blinking. The wolf pack hauled people out of their cars, lined them up with their hands in the air, and machine gunned them with the harsh lights from the head beams of the patrol cars.

Unemployment rose sky high.

The police nicknamed themselves the Gestapo.

Still the brown refugees came from behind the cotton curtain, flooding through the gates of the city down at Union Station and the bus depots on Fifth Street.

The police roamed Soulville lining people up against the walls and shaking them down.

Still the people came.

They knocked Mill Creek down around them, and moved the old slum dwellers out west into new slums, and the cotton country refugees poured into the crumbling slums that had been vacated.

Rooming-house fires burned them up, police dogs mauled them, restaurants refused them service, schools refused to teach them, native St. Louisans snubbed them, politicians, and businessmen, and corner boys, and police officers fleeced them, but still they came.

In a city of 750,000 people they swelled the ranks of Soulville to 300,000 strong.

Some of them came out to the Golden Trumpet where the Splib Band was holding down a six-nighter. They wrote their friends and relatives about it. That's how the news reached the cotton country, news that stirred things up the way nothing had since Florence Mills's death over thirty years ago.

Jerome decided to invest $800 and back a record for them. The record was called "Half Free," and had lyrics on it written by Raymond and sung by Lobo. On the flip side was an original dip into the nut bag by Raymond called "Falling Down" in which the chord progressions were based on "London Bridge," but rearranged to emphasize an eerie, militant rhythm section laying down a gutbucket beat in seven-eight time. The record moved real big across town and then took off across the nation behind the disc jockey code of two local stations who featured only rhythm and blues and jazz on their programs.

"Hey, now don't y'all get too hard on the gray boy," Wilbur told them one night, after the request for "Half Free" had come up for the third straight show. "I mean some of 'em are all right. One of the few cats I could get to help back me, so I could open up, was an ofay cat I played with in the Ernie Fergen band and he's got a one-fourth interest in this joint."

Lobo smiled at Wilbur and went back into the song everybody was requesting, "Well, you had a good home, but you left."

"That's right!"

"Yeh, baby, you had a good home, but you made it."

"Aw yeh."

"Now you gonna regret the day that you left, for the rest of the days of your life."

"Sure will now!"

"From Africa."

"Uh-huh."

"From Africa."

"Aw yeh, baby, when you left Africa you goofed, man," somebody said.

"And now you just half free."

"Yeh."

"Half free," Lobo said.

"That's right."

"Half free, that's all, that's all, that's all. In the great big beautiful land of liberty."

They clapped, they yelled, they cheered him on.

Now, ole Charlie was there when you left.
Aw yeh, Charlie was there when you made it, baby.
And now you gonna regret the day he came,
For the rest of the days of your life.
See 'cause now you just half free.
All over the world you just half free.
Half free, that's all, that's all, that's all.
In this great big land of liberty.

Now ain't no need of feeling blue,
'Cause Charlie got your woman and yo money too,
See that happened in slavery,
Aw man, that slavery was really something, Jim,
Yeh, and now you still just half free.
Half free boy, that's all, that's all, that's all,
See that's the reason we call you boy,
In this great big land of liberty?

Well, now ain't no sense in going to school,
You do that you break ole Charlie's rule,
And see ain't no sense in you doing that,
Now I'm here to tell you baby, that's not where it's at.
See, you just half free.
Now you got to get used to that baby, you half free.
Half free, that's all, man, that's all.
In the great big land of liberty.

Well, now ain't no need in trying to vote,
See you do that you might get a rope round yo throat,
And like ain't no sense in trying to eat,
'Cause you do that you might get knocked off your feet,
Baby I keep trying to tell you you just half free.
That's all you are baby, you just half free.

Half free, that's all, that's all,
In the great big beautiful land of liberty.

Well, now one of these days I'ma be all free.

"Yeh, sing it, Lobo!"

"You hear me? I say one of these days I'ma be all free."

"Yeh!"

"I say one of these days I'ma be all free!"

"Yeh, or there ain't gone be no land of liberty," they said finishing it for him.

"I say one of these days I'ma be—"

"All free!"

"Yeh, one of these days we gone be—"

"All free!"

"Oh yeh, one of these days we gone be—"

"All free!"

"Aw ye-aaah! Or there ain't gonna be no la-aaaand of lib-beeer-teeeeeeeeeey!"

Lobo brought the house down. That was the same night Teacher got up on the stand and got into the act.

"Hey, brothers and sisters," Teacher said during the jam session hour. "Welcome to the Golden Trumpet. Brother and sisters, you dig that?"

They chuckled.

"Aw come on now, you know who I'm talking 'bout. I'm talking 'bout all you club members out there with the pretty brown skin, yeh."

They laughed.

"Yeh, and to those of you out there who ain't club members, welcome to you too."

That brought some nervous smiles.

"See it's all right, we don't mind y'all coming in and socializing with us. We're not prejudiced."

The smiles got more nervous.

"Yeh, you know it's kind of early in the wee hours, you know around that midnight hour, when the man gets kind of mean out there in those streets, and I know you know what I mean if you're a member and if you ain't a member you got a good idea of what I'm talking about anyway." Teacher cleared his throat. "Yeh," he said. "So do me a favor and be careful, will you? See, 'cause that man's out of sight. Like you take the other day, there I was standing on the corner waiting for a service car and the man pulled up in his squad car and jumped out. Hey, boy, he said." Teacher looked around on the stage as though he was trying to find out whom the cop was talking to. That was good for a laugh.

"Hey, boy?" Teacher continued looking around. "You talking to me, man? I told the cat. Yeh, you, the stud said." Teacher stuck a thumb in his chest. "You dig that, the cat was actually talking to me."

They chuckled.

"Look man, I told him. Now I know you're supposed to be Tarzan, but I mean, I ain't your son."

They hollered.

"Aw, you're one of those wise guys, my man said. You ever been arrested before?"

Teacher reared back as though he was being shocked off his feet. "Have I ever been arrested before, you kidding? Man, you ever heard of a brown-skin club member who ain't never been arrested before?"

They roared.

"What for? my man wanted to know."

Teacher jerked his head as though the cop was slapping him in the face with words and they giggled.

"What for, man, you kidding? Lots of things, man, lots of things."

The drummer hit a few licks on the drum to emphasize Teacher's last line.

"Like what, for instance?"

The way Teacher looked made the crowd laugh. "Aw man,

man," Teacher said as though he was wondering if the policeman had come from another planet, or something. "Like waiting on the corner to catch a service car for instance, or trying to go to school to get an education, or trying to get a decent job to support my family, or trying to vote, or asking for equal rights, or trying to get cats like you to keep their hands off my women—"

Every woman in the house laughed.

"But mainly for standing up here filling you in on why I've ever been arrested before like I'm trying to explain to you now," Teacher said.

They screamed, they cheered, they laughed so hard tears rolled down their cheeks.

Well, kiss my wrist, Raymond thought. Now he's a goddamn comedian.

The crowd agreed with him.

ABOUT A MONTH after Raymond added Teacher to the show, Lobo invited Lorraine Jordan up on the stand in the middle of the show.

"Say, man, what you doing?" Raymond wanted to know.

He found out soon enough. Lobo announced over the mike that Lorraine was going to sing the lyrics she had written to a tune called "Country" which Raymond had written and had the band playing for the last few months. Now it was Raymond's turn to shrug when somebody brought something new up on the stand.

"Country" was a tricky blues written in five-four time where the drummer broke the rhythm all the way through and the horns kept the beat going. It was a tune where the piano man played outside and left the bass player driving like mad combing in the gaps. "Country" was a tune that called for more precision and timing than a drill team performing closed-ranks exercises with naked bayonets extended on the end of their rifles. That's why raised eyebrows went up in the band when Lobo made his announcement.

Eyes popped in the audience too, once Lorraine started singing. Lorraine was riding in between the horns and piano, singing the notes the bass player was laying down. That cracked the band up.

Raymond and Lobo got into it after it was all over, because he wouldn't hire Lorraine for the show.

"Lorraine ain't good enough, huh?"

"I didn't say that."

"Yeh, okay, man, that's okay."

"We got enough of everything we need right now," Raymond said. "Now later on it might be a different story."

"Yeh, okay man, I said okay," Lobo said.

16

. . . don't ask for no sympathy . . .

TEACHER MARRIED INEZ two weeks before they were scheduled to take off on a southern tour that would take them as far west as Los Angeles before they headed back toward home again. He got his beard trimmed down to where it covered only his chin, like the rest of the band members, and they teased him about that all the time.

Then it happened, what they had been expecting to happen ever since they had started performing at the Golden Trumpet. The man moved in on the set one night and told Raymond he was busted and that the show was over.

Raymond and Lobo knew who the man was. It was Pezzarus.

"Right now, we'd like to take a brief little intermission," Raymond told the crowd who were wondering what the hell was going on.

Pezzarus snatched the microphone out of Raymond's hand. "You won't be coming back," Pezzarus told him.

"Man, dig him," Teacher said. "The fuzz is been studying James Cagney."

That didn't get any laughs.

"Don't worry," Jerome told Raymond. "I'll go your bail."

It seemed Pezzarus had found a roach in Raymond's car. He made the mistake of telling where in the car he had found it.

"Man, you got the wrong cat," Mickey said. "The roach is mine."

"Naw, Mickey, I can't let you do that. The roach is mine," Teacher said.

"Let's go, Douglas."

"Now wait a minute, man, how you know it belongs to Raymond?" Wilbur said.

"Look, mister, all I know is we found some dope in Douglas's car and we're taking him down."

"You call that possession?" Jerome wanted to know.

"It's a tech," Raymond said.

"Yeh, I'm hip. It's a drag, that's really what you mean," Jerome said.

"Look Jim, like I told you before it's my roach," Mickey said.

"Naw, man, it's mine," Teacher insisted.

"Man, you don't have to prove nothing to me just 'cause you got married. I said it was mine, didn't I?" Mickey held up his arm so Pezzarus could see. "Look man I'm a junkie and I'm confessing for all my crimes so why don't you take me on down and get it over with?"

They all got weak in the knees, Mickey doing that.

"Okay, since you feel that way about it, you can come too," Pezzarus said.

"Naw, man, you got to make up your mind who you want. You can't get but one stud on that roach," Teacher told him. "So just make up your little white mind which one it's gonna be."

Pezzarus turned red. The blond cop, standing silently at his side, did too.

"What's wrong with you people?" Pezzarus said.

"Nothing man, we just sick of studs like you taking us through them changes all the time," Raymond told him.

"Yeh, and I can tell you right now, you're gonna have a hell of a time proving that roach belongs to my nephew," Wilbur said.

"You guys really think you're something, don't you?" Pezzarus said, putting his hands on his hips. "I heard that crap you were pulling up there on the bandstand. I oughta run the rest of y'all in on that."

"Now we're getting to it," Teacher said. "You don't dig the message we're putting down. Well, you want to know something, man? We don't give a damn what you dig, so if you want to run us in for that, go ahead."

"All just because we're down here all alone in a colored neighborhood you're trying to give us a hard time," Pezzarus said, "but I can tell you now it ain't gonna work."

"Naw, man, we ain't trying to do nothing but keep you from trying to whip them fancy games on us all the time," Jerome said.

"Yeh, well if he's so dead set on taking me in, let him," Raymond said.

"Naw man, y'all supposed to be heading south tomorrow and the band can't go without you, Raymond. Like I said, man, take me down."

"Aw Mickey, why'd you have to put yourself on the spot? Nobody had nothing on you," Jerome said.

"Aw it's about time I went to take the cure anyway," Mickey said.

"I said I wanted Douglas."

"Yeh, well let me run something down for you, man. You think you can get me on a roach go ahead and try, but I'm telling you right now, I'm suing. I'm fighting this game all the way, 'cause I'm tired of studs like you fugging with me, so you want to make it hard for me, go ahead, 'cause I'm damn sure coming right back to make it hard on you."

"What's all that supposed to mean?"

"Take me down and find out."

"Aw, forget it, Sarge, it ain't worth it," the blond cop said. "Let's take the junkie and let it go at that; we're wasting a lot of time."

Pezzarus looked over the whole crowd. There was murder in Lobo's eyes.

"Ah, you got away this time, but I'll get you, you and your buddies too, especially that paroled cop-killing son-of-a-bitching buddy of yours there," Pezzarus said. "I'm gonna put all your kind behind locked doors before I'm through."

Lobo started moving toward Pezzarus, and Pezzarus went for his gun.

"You ever hear of Ugo?" Raymond said, holding Lobo back.

"Ugo? Ugo who?"

"Ugo screw yourself, flatfoot," Raymond told him.

They never did get straight on who the roach belonged to.

. . . but, if it's not asking too much . . .

JEROME WENT WITH THEM as band manager, and since it was his dough that had got them started nobody objected to his cutting himself in for a bigger share once the group had started to make money. The band members were afraid it wouldn't last, but Raymond knew better. The band didn't have any financial worries and he knew it. By the time they came off the tour Jerome would have grass customers halfway across the country. So finance was no problem. The group could play what they wanted to play, say what they wanted to say, and not have to worry about whether the public would go for it or not, because the band was a perfect front for Jerome's business and as long as business was good, Jerome would be willing to pick up the tab. As things turned out, picking up the tab wasn't necessary.

They played to a Standing Room Only crowd in Kansas City and police had to be called out to control the people who couldn't get in.

In Little Rock, Arkansas, the people got so enthusiastic over Lobo singing "Half Free" that the authorities claimed the overflowing crowd had gotten out of hand, and canceled the second show. In Biloxi, Mississippi, they went wild over Teacher and the engagement got extended for three days, but they only played one, because the sheriff ordered them out of town.

The sepia press got wind of them in Oklahoma City after a review of their performance appeared in the *Muskogee Black Messenger*.

. . . there is a modern-day Moses among the Negro people today [the American Negro Press Association said]. He is more powerful than any Jack Johnson, Florence Mills, or Joe Louis, for he is a people's spokesman, but not like Frederick Douglas, or Booker Washington, no glib-tongued orator he, but he is the gauge of the people and wherever he goes they come out to see him, for he has come into their hearts through the blues, a medium they understand; his rod is a golden trumpet and when he puts it to his lips and speaks they listen for the walls of Jericho to come tumbling down, believing he can roll back the Red Sea and lead them to the Promised Land. This man, this nondescript jazz musician, resurrected from the tomb of obscurity, has suddenly burst upon the American scene like a human atomic bomb radiating hope, determination, and direc-

tion on a disheartened people who never knew what it meant to be told they were somebody until he came along . . .

The white press ignored him, but the magical spell the Splib Band was weaving was too powerful to go unchallenged and local imitators sprang up in the cities he appeared in. One of those imitators hit the headlines of the daily papers with a bang.

BAND LEADER JAILED FOR JAZZING UP
STAR-SPANGLED BANNER

Jimmy Parker's picture made all the papers. So did the lyrics he had sung before a huge crowd in Houston.

Ofay, can you see, any bedbugs on me. If you do, take a few, 'cause I got them from you!

The FBI came down to look over Raymond's show in Shreveport, Louisiana, he was barred from New Orleans, and Dallas called out special guards on the night he held his show there. And another thing happened; people began treating him as though he was some kind of leader other than the band leader he was supposed to be.

It was on the trip back through Los Angeles, after playing Spokane and Frisco, that he ran into real trouble, out at the Palladium before a house full of people. The trouble presented itself in the form of a chocolate-bronze woman in a tight-fitting red dress.

Raymond, Charles, Douglas, he saw her lips say.

He almost fell off the bandstand. Well, I'll be damn, Codene McCluskey. Who would have ever thought he would run into her again?

18

THEY GOT HIGH and she told him about her two marriages which hadn't worked out.

"I tried it once myself," Raymond said.

"I know. I heard about it. I know it might sound terrible to say it, but I'm glad you're not still married to Jetan, although I am sorry she's dead."

She asked him about Teacher's wife, Inez. "Teacher's really changed, hasn't he?"

"Yeh," Raymond said. "In some ways, but in other ways he's just the same."

Codene and Teacher hadn't had much to say to each other. "I don't think he ever got over the fact that me and you used to go together," she told him.

Raymond told her how Teacher had warned him he would soon be a marked man in America and how the people in power would be out to get him. "I wish I could take you with me," he said, "but it wouldn't be fair."

"We don't have much time left before your bus leaves," she said. "Let's not waste it."

19

OTHING WENT RIGHT for him after that; at least that was the way it seemed to Raymond. The band grew in popularity, but he became dissatisfied with his performances, and not only that, but the police started riding him everywhere he and the band appeared, just as Teacher had predicted. By the time they got back to St. Louis in the spring of '60 things were really hot for them.

BLACK SUPREMIST BACK IN TOWN!
DOUGLAS BACK IN CITY WITH RABBLE-ROUSING SHOW!

That's how the sepia press welcomed him back to the city. The sepia press talked about the things that had happened at the places they played. One of the papers linked all the picketings, race riots, sit-ins, and lawsuits that had occurred in the country in 1960 to the fact that the Splib Band had played in those cities before the fireworks began.

Whenever his band appeared in a town, groups would come out to meet him during a show and ask his advice on local racial problems. As a result he had been forced to spend more and more time studying history and law, and less on music. This was something that really bugged him, but he had found out to his dismay that once the people chose you as their spokesman you couldn't step down, you couldn't deviate, you couldn't take one step backwards, because you were looked up to as the champ and the champ was required to carry the battle into the enemy's country. And not only that, but you could speak out on the things the people wanted you to talk about and get drug by cats like the Muslims, who called him an Uncle Tom for not being outspoken enough, and studs like Teacher who'd had a fit because he told the people down there in

Houston, Texas, that Parker had gone too far in saying what he had about the "Star-Spangled Banner."

"Man, I never thought I'd live to see the day when you'd do that," Teacher had said.

"Look man, like they got brown studs in this world who do things they ain't got no business doing too."

"I never said they didn't."

"And like everything, brown ain't necessarily good and everything white ain't necessarily bad."

"I'll go along with the brown," Teacher said.

"Man, you ain't right about everything."

"I'm right about ofays, man, they're a decadent race, and they're going to wind up getting exterminated no matter what you, or me, or anybody else over here has to say about it, so why waste your time taking up for them? Look man, you can't turn back the tide of history, Jim."

"And you can't direct the course of it. No man can."

"What makes you so sure, man?"

"Well, I'll tell you one thing I'm sure of. You're a man and not a god. And you ain't running nothing too much down here on this earth except your own big mouth," Raymond said.

"Aw, is that right, man?"

"Yeh, man. You damn right. Like I know you're heavy and all that, but like this is my band, and I am supposed to be the leader of the show, so I don't see why you should be getting all upset about the way I'm doing things as long as we keep breaking even in the box office and you get your cut."

"Wow, baby, you really taking yourself seriously these days, ain't you?"

"Naw, man, but I ain't letting nobody try to lord it over nobody all the time like you do either."

"Aw, is that what I'm trying to do, man?"

"Man, I don't know what the hell you're trying to do, but I do know one thing, if you got any ideas about running this show you might as well just get them out your mind now."

"Wow, man, it sounds to me like you're suffering from delusions of grandeur."

"You go to hell," Raymond told him. "I don't have to be wrong all the time, just because I don't happen to agree with everything you say."

"I never said you did."

"You implied it."

"Did I?"

"Damn right, and anyway, man, if you're so right about everything all the time, how come you ain't running things then?"

"Who says I ain't running things, man?"

"Aw Jim, you can talk crazy all you want to, but I'ma tell you like you told me. All you have to do to be a success in this world is to find out what makes a thing behave the way it does, why, and apply the principle."

"I'm hip."

"Yeh, well it looks to me like I've done just a little bit better job of applying myself than you have."

Teacher looked at him, his eyes dead-flat. "What makes you so sure?" he had answered.

He hadn't been able to sleep at night since then. He'd wake up in the middle of the night having nightmares after what Teacher had said. Damn man, what if Teacher was right; what if what Teacher had said really was true? Damn.

20

THE WHOLE WEEK they gigged down at the Golden Trumpet to turn-away crowds he thought about it, and early in the morning, just before they pulled out of town on another tour, he went running over to Argustus's like a little boy who had met up with somebody who acted like they knew a hell of a lot more than he did about something that was very important to him.

"What the hell, boy," Argustus complained. "What you mean coming over here at four o'clock in the morning and dragging me out of bed?"

"Sorry, Grandpa, but there's something I gotta know, and I figured if anybody around here knew, you would."

"Aw yeh," Argustus said, his left eyebrow slanting up over his forehead. "It's like that, huh?"

"Yeh."

Argustus stretched and got out of bed. "Ida!"

"I already got coffee on," Ida answered from the kitchen.

Argustus motioned Raymond to follow him into the living room and they sat down on the green davenport that Raymond used to sit on and practice his trumpet when he was still in high school.

"What's her name?"

"Naw, Grandpa, it ain't like that."

"Aw boy, who you kidding? You wouldn't come busting over here this time of morning unless some dame has gotten you all screwed up in the head, so come on off it now and just tell me the chick's name."

"Aw, well the same one that I brought over here one night to hear us practicing, but I didn't come over here to ask you nothing about her."

"Uh-huh. The real stacked one, huh, that was so crazy about you. Well, a guy could do worse."

"She wasn't crazy about me."

"Who you kidding? What's that gal's name, Flourine, or was it Morphine?"

"Codene," Raymond said, his temper rising.

Argustus laughed. "Yeh, that's it, Codene. I knew her name sounded like one of them toothpastes."

"Yeh."

"Yeh," Argustus said. "Look boy, there was my own Lindy who was your grandmother and now Ida there, so I know a thing or two about women who want to marry a guy who ain't exactly got his mind set on settling down," Argustus told him. "Besides, you know ole Wilbur had his troubles with that chick named Marsha, and they ain't got married yet, which is got a lot to do with the way he is today."

"He's doing all right, ain't he?"

Argustus shrugged. "He is career-wise if that's what you mean, and he's really raking in the dough, but he ain't satisfied although he pretends hard enough."

"He ain't, huh?" Raymond said.

"Uh-uh. Naw boy, no man is complete without his woman," Argustus said, "and sometimes I think Wilbur opened that place with the hope that Marsha would drop in from out of nowhere one of these days after hearing about him being there. You know they lost track of each other after he got out of the Army."

"Aw yeh."

"Yeh," Argustus said. "And now you take your father and Mae, there's another good example of what I'm talking about."

"How you mean, Grandpa?"

"Well just look how your father changed when he lost your mother."

"Aw, I don't think he changed so much."

"He's changed," Argustus said. "He ain't trying no more. Your old man was a hell of a guy once."

"How you mean trying?"

"Trying to better his condition, or see to it that you two kids better yours. You ain't never seen him at any of your public performances, have you?"

"Naw, but I thought that was because of that little tiff we had when I cut out from home."

Argustus shook his head. "Naw, and he didn't show for Helen's graduation from college either. Naw he just don't give a damn no more, not like he used to anyway."

Raymond tried to fill Argustus in on what was happening between him and Codene, but he didn't do a very good job of it.

"Boy, you know what?" Argustus said, dragging some smoke

rings through a short, stubby pipe. "If I was you I'd head dead back to California the first chance I got and marry that gal. 'Course now, I ain't you, but if I was, that's what I'd do."

"Aw, Grandpa, I couldn't do that."

"Why not?"

"Well, that's what I wanted to talk to you about in the first place," Raymond told him.

Ida brought them in some coffee and Raymond told him about what Teacher had said, and how he figured maybe Teacher could really be right. " 'Cause I mean, hell, Grandpa I ain't never really known no white studs except in an acquaintance kind of way, and I had some broads, but you know you can't never tell nothing by them 'cause a woman's always gonna put up a front."

"You mean everybody's gonna always put up a front if they can do it and get away with it," Argustus said.

"Well, yeh, that's what I mean, so how can you really tell where the hell they're at?" Raymond said.

Argustus cleared his throat. "Boy you done really got yourself into something these days, ain't you."

"Aw, I ain't into that much."

"The hell you ain't. You know I once had to make up my mind about something like that too, back there when that thing blew off over in East St. Louis that time," Argustus said.

"What thing?"

"Never you mind, I done said too much about it already. Look, boy, people are people and all people are animals, now don't you ever forget that, 'cause if you do you're in a world of trouble. *All* people are animals," Argustus said, "no matter whether they're black, white, blue or polka-dot green, they're all animals, civilized maybe, but animals with the same instincts, desires, and needs of the beasts that roam through the jungle."

"Aw yeh?"

"Yeh," Argustus told him. "That's why you've got to learn how to look out for yourself, because they'll all get you if they can; that's animal nature. That's why you got to watch everybody, especially your own kind, because they know your habits and weaknesses better than anybody else and that's why they can get to you quicker and better than anybody else."

"Yeh, well I suppose you got a point, but—"

"Ain't no buts. Look, boy, the only reason I'm telling you this is because I see them pushing you out there and I know what can happen behind your back, so this is something you need to know in order to stay alive and maybe really do something worthwhile for this ignorant, stupid, don't-give-a-damn bunch of bastards known as Negroes in this country," Argustus said.

"Yeh, Grandpa, I guess, but—"

"What I tell you about them buts?" Argustus said.

"Well, what I mean—"

"Well hell, look boy, do me a favor, marry the broad, raise you some kids, save you some money, tell Teacher to go to hell, and get out of here and let me get back to sleep. Hell, I ain't as young as I used to be," Argustus told him.

Ida made him drink another cup of coffee before she would let him go home.

When he got home he woke up Hosea and Wilbur and they had a long discussion that lasted all the way up to eight o'clock in the morning when he had to leave with the band on another tour.

. . . Please send me someone to love . . .

ON THE ROAD Raymond and Teacher got into it again, because Raymond wanted Teacher and Lobo to tame down their material a little.

"Ain't no sense in insulting everybody just 'cause you got a boss message to deliver," Raymond told them.

"Wow, man, this stud's fair turning out to be a Tom," Teacher said.

"Yeh, man, your feathers are starting to show," Lobo told him.

"You're a hell of a cat to be calling somebody chicken after what you did over on Garfield that time," Raymond said to Teacher.

"Yeh, man, well I didn't know no better then, but it's different now."

Raymond laughed.

"Go to hell," Teacher said. "I'ma do my material the same way I've always done it and if you don't like it you know what you can do."

"Yeh, me too," Lobo said. "I didn't spend twelve years in the joint just to come out and be polite to folks just because you feel like the dirty bastards are getting their feelings hurt."

"Well, if you're going to keep working in this show you're going to tone your material down," Raymond told them.

"Man, dig this cat."

"Man, this cat really thinks he's something, don't he? I guess I'ma have to knock him on his ass," Lobo said.

"Not if I can help it," Raymond told him.

Lobo tried staring Raymond down, the way he used to do in the old days, but that didn't work.

"Aw man, you know I can kick your ass any time I get ready," Lobo said.

"Man, I don't know nothing."

"Yeh, I guess you forgot."

"I ain't never known it," Raymond told him.

"Man, if this nigger was a white man I'd hang his ass," Lobo said.

Teacher didn't say anything.

"Aw you mother—"

Lobo swung on Raymond and knocked him clear across the room.

Red rings of anger swelled in Raymond's head. His grandfather had warned him. His grandfather had warned him and he had left himself wide open to be hit upside the head like a chump anyway. He should have learned his lesson a long time ago when those studs had ganged him that night on Garfield.

Lobo charged across the room at Raymond and met a round-house right that landed dead in his eyes. That stopped him for a second or two as his eye started ballooning out of shape, and the realization dawned on him that Raymond would actually fight him back. They started moving in circles around each other looking for an opening.

Lobo brought a knee up for Raymond's groin and Raymond sidestepped the way he used to on the football field and stiff-armed Lobo's face down onto the floor where he picked up a few splinters.

When Lobo got up he brought a wooden chair up with him and smashed it across Raymond's shoulder before he could get out of the way, and as Raymond was heading toward the floor he drove his foot at his groin and the point of his shoe sunk into Raymond's hip as he turned his body out of the way. Lobo managed to kick him a couple of times in the ribs before Raymond could roll out of the way and get back on his feet, and if it hadn't been for the management calling the police, one of them might actually have killed the other. After the police had restrained them long enough for them to cool down, they both looked around for Teacher. Teacher was gone.

The police didn't see anything for Raymond to be grinning about. Neither did Lobo, who left the show for good after it was decided that neither of them wanted to prosecute. The sepia weeklies didn't miss it.

SPLIB BAND MEMBERS SPLIT!
OKLAHOMA THEATER CANCELS SPLIB SHOW!
BAND LEADER AND MEMBER IN BRAWL!

Teacher grew a full beard, wrapped a turban around his head, called himself the Messiah and Lobo and the rest of the performers on his show the Disciples. The white dailies picked that up.

219

No one picked up the heartache Raymond felt after losing life-long friends. Even Inez was against him now. That tore him up inside, but he remembered what his grandfather said and just kept plugging ahead. Lorraine was glad to join the show, and he knew the band members dug it because of the way they teased her about being the only member of the show who wasn't wearing a beard.

They headed west. They traveled west and the people came out to see them. The people brought him their problems. The people pushed him out on that limb all alone by himself.

"Hey Jerome, how come you stuck with me instead of splitting with Lobo and Teacher?" Raymond asked him one day.

"You kidding? Man, your group's gonna make a hell of a lot more bread than Teacher's ever will, and besides I got my business contacts set up through this outfit. I ain't about to go through all the trouble of setting them up all over again."

His grandpa sure was a wise old stud. Raymond cut loose one of his sad smiles.

That left only Codene.

22

SHE STOOD in the red dress, he said he dug her in, and peered into the fading sunset for a sign of the Splib bus on the Freeway. The Freeway was a crawling mass of metallic blurs whizzing along bumper to bumper far as the eye could see.

The bus was a half hour late now and she began to wonder if it would really come. She had only his letter to go on and the memory of the last night he had been in L.A. She still had the impression he was more interested in blowing his horn than he was in making love to her. Well, they said that was the price you paid if you were foolish enough to fall for an artist. Everyone knew art came first with an artist. Not even a woman could fight that. She was a fool. Suppose the government locked him up after he made his appearance before the Senate Sub-committee investigating subversive activities in the entertainment profession? Suppose she was left to bring up the children she would give him alone, and at her age too, while he was rotting away in jail somewhere, or worse, dead?

She smoothed down the skirt that the warm wind kept hiking above her knees.

Off in the distance the sun dipped like an orange beacon into the California foothills. She gazed into the foothills a long time before the Splib bus appeared.

Raymond Charles Douglas. She gave his name to the wind. She was scared to death, but she would never let him know it, and a few minutes later when he started the steep climb from the highway, up to where she was standing, she waved at him.

Raymond Charles Douglas, her lips said silently.

He hurried.

HPL
Genre Lists
African American Fiction